HEIR
OF
MYSTERY

The Second Unlikely Exploit

HEIR OF MYSTERY

~~~ *or* ~~~

FOUR LEGS GOOD

PHILIP ARDAGH

with illustrations by David Roberts

SCHOLASTIC INC.

New York   Toronto   London   Auckland   Sydney
Mexico City   New Delhi   Hong Kong   Buenos Aires

ISBN 0-439-73017-1

Text copyright © 2003 by Philip Ardagh
Illustrations copyright © 2003 by David Roberts
All rights reserved. Published by Scholastic Inc., by arrangement with Henry Holt and Company, LLC. SCHOLASTIC and associated logos are trademarks and/or registered trademarks of Scholastic Inc.

First published in the United States in 2004 by Henry Holt and Company, LLC. Originally published in Great Britain in 2003 by Faber and Faber Ltd.

All rights reserved.
Published by Scholastic Inc., 557 Broadway, New York, NY 10012, by arrangement with Henry Holt and Company, LLC.

12 11 10 9 8 7 6 5 4 3 2 1   5 6 7 8 9 10/0
Printed in the U.S.A.   40

First Scholastic paperback printing, December 2005

~~~

To Tim and Bradley of the Sussex Ambulance
Service and to the doctors, nurses, and auxiliary staff
of the Coronary Care Unit at Conquest Hospital, all
of whose acquaintance I unexpectedly made when
reaching the closing stages of this book.

A heartfelt thank-you.

~~~

A Word to the Wise

There are more good people in this world than bad. You may not think so, but it's true. The bad ones make a lot of noise and cause a lot of trouble, so they're the ones we see on the news and portrayed in books and movies, but your average human being is a good human being. And that's a fact.

Although it's always important to be careful in life, from whom to trust to what time you walk home on your own, it's also important to remember this. Sure, the guy who saves you from drowning *might* be planning to shave off your hair and sell it as a wig, but more likely than not he's simply trying to save your life. If most people were bad, nothing would ever get done. There would be no such thing as society. So be alert, yes. Be sensible, yes. But try not to be afraid. If you're afraid, you're letting the bad guys win.

—PHILIP ARDAGH

"Anything awful makes me laugh.
I misbehaved once at a funeral."

—Charles Lamb
From a letter dated August 9, 1815

PROLOGUE

THINGS TO DO TODAY

Get up ✓
Wash and brush teeth ✓
Get dressed ✓
Feed cats ✓
Empty dishwasher ✓
Have 1st cup of coffee ✓
Read mail ✓
Check answering machine for messages ✓
Check e-mail ✓
Have 2nd cup of coffee ✓
Write HEIR OF MYSTERY

MUST DO!!!!

Watch TV
Feed cats
Have supper
Wash and brush teeth
Go to bed

CHAPTER ONE

First and foremost, this is a book about death. Okay, so it doesn't start with an actual death like the Unlikely Exploit that precedes it (with young Fergal McNally hurtling out of an open window, the wind whistling past his sticky-out ears), but you'll find a lot of it about. Life's like that, though, I'm afraid. Then again, if we didn't have death, this little planet that we call home would be a very over-crowded place. Not only that, most buildings would be old people's homes and entire continents would be taken up with retirement village after retirement village, populated by some very old and very wrinkled people indeed. On your birthday, you wouldn't only get a card from your grandparents but also your great-grandparents and great-great-grandparents and so on and so on, all the way back to some couple (looking suspiciously like close relatives of apes, if Charlie Darwin is to be believed) whose idea of a fun day out is hunting and gathering and whose idea of a card might be a particularly interesting leaf, folded in half, with a sooty smudge on the front. If you thought your gran's mustache tickled, just imagine one of them trying to plant a slobbering kiss on you. So death is not only the opposite of life, it's also an important part of it . . . or, to be more accurate, an important part of the circle of life, which is more than just a theme in Walt Disney's *The Lion King*. People are born. People grow up. People have children. People grow old. People die. People's children grow up and have children and they die, and so the big wheel keeps on turning. The sad part is when the circle is interrupted. Fergal McNally didn't even finish the growing-up stage, which understandably upset his sisters, Jackie and Le Fay, and his brothers, Albion and Joshua (a.k.a. Albie and Josh, or the twins), and a significant number of people in this exploit don't reach the growing-old stage. I'm sorry, but there it is. As I began by saying, some three hundred and fifty-one words ago, first and foremost this book is about death.

In addition to death, you're also about to encounter a lot of rain. Like death, rain has its uses. Without rain, most—if not all—plant life would die, there'd be one long drought, and eventually all the animals and humans would die too, so we should be offering a great big cheery THANK-YOU to our local rain gods or to the God of Everything or to Mother Nature (or whichever, if any, deity handles these things). That doesn't mean to say we have to like rain. (I'm glad we have electricity—it's very useful—but I don't particularly want to hug it. Hug a big piece of electricity and it'll burn you to a crisp.) I like the different seasons. I like summer to be sunny and winter to be snowy. I like the crispy golden leaves of autumn and fresh green shoots of spring. I feel sorry for people who live in brilliant sunshine all year round. B-O-R-I-N-G! Rain plays its part in making the seasons individual. But the rain in this book is a merciless rain. It's torrential— which is why it comes down in torrents—and it's cold and seemingly never-ending.

The night this particular Unlikely Exploit began, it was raining in Fishbone Forest, a forest that gets its name from the shape of its trees. Huge, pineless firs, they look like the skeletons of long-dead fishes, their noses to the ground. Wrought-iron railings run all the way around the huge forest, with four great gateways, one at each of the four main points of the compass. The gates are always locked. These have always been a puzzle to the local people, who believe that no one in their right mind would want to go into the forest anyway. What they don't realize is that they're there to keep *things* in, not people out.

And the rain? This was the kind of rain that would have to be painted with great slashes across a canvas with lashings of paint. This was the kind of rain that soaked your clothes into a soggy mass in under a minute and then continued to beat down on you. This was the kind of rain that made you think that it had something *personal* against you!

It was through this downpour that an old van, the color of English mustard, was driving up to the West Gate of Fishbone Forest. At the wheel was a small man. He was a very small man. In fact, he was as small as the small

masked burglar at the end of the first Unlikely Exploit. Okay, okay, so he *was* the small masked burglar at the end of the first Unlikely Exploit, which means the first time we met him he was stealing a human brain in a jar of pickling vinegar from Sacred Heart Hospital.

The small masked burglar was no longer masked, but he was still small and did have a name. That name was Stefan Multachan, which sounds rather grand, but because he wasn't, everyone who knew him called him "Mulch." The only time he was ever addressed as Mr. Multachan was when he was sent junk mail—*Dear Mr. Multachan: You're already halfway toward winning the vacation of a lifetime; You're a guaranteed winner*—or when he was caught doing a burglary: "Stefan Multachan, we find you guilty of stealing the bag of newts from Wilf's Fish Emporium and sentence you to two weeks' hard labor and ban you from keeping amphibians for six months. . . ." You get the picture.

The human brain Mulch had stolen was still in its jar of pickling vinegar, now wrapped up in brown parcel paper—the good thick stuff—and was sitting on the passenger seat beside him. Brains weren't usually kept in pickling vinegar at Sacred Heart. They were usually kept in formaldehyde or a formaldehyde solution, but for reasons far too time-consuming to relate now, this particular brain ended up in pickling vinegar from nearby Ma's Pickling Store. (The "Ma" in question was actually one Mrs. Edna Bloinstein and, unusually for a "ma," I'd say, she'd never had any children.) This particular brain belonged to Fergal McNally, whom I mentioned earlier.

Well, the brain couldn't really belong to Fergal McNally because Fergal McNally was dead. What I meant to say was that it had been Fergal's brain. It was the brain *of* the dead Fergal. If you could see through the darkness, through the rain, through the side of the English-mustard-colored van, and through the brown parcel paper—the good thick stuff—you would see the word JUVENILE written on the label beneath Fergal's name. That's because Fergal was just a little kid when he fell out of a fourteenth-story window and landed splat on the pavement below.

Of course, Fergal's family had no idea that Fergal's brain had been removed from his dead body—though it's standard procedure for a postmortem, carried out to try to find the cause of death—let alone put in a jar of pickling vinegar, let alone stolen by Mulch, wrapped in brown paper, and driven to the West Gate of Fishbone

Forest. In fact, the dead boy's two sisters (Jackie and Le Fay, remember) and two twin brothers (Joshua and Albion, need I remind you) were, at that very moment, being driven home to their father to break the news of the terrible accident.

Mulch drew the van to a halt and managed to struggle into a bright yellow plastic raincoat and matching hat before opening the door to the rain. The sound of the rain on the plastic sounded like he was being hit with a million tiny Ping-Pong balls, and the water ran off the brim of the hat like a waterfall. Mulch's hands were soaked as he produced a large, old-fashioned key from his pocket and put it in the lock of the gate. The mechanism was well oiled and the key turned with ease.

Mulch pulled both gates open wide, the rain splashing in his face making it hard to see, and leapt back into

the van. He drove into the forest, parked again, and dashed out to close and lock the West Gate behind him. There was a flash of sheet lightning; in other words, not the forked lightning of horror movies, which often hits branches and sets them alight, but the type of lightning that seems to light up the whole sky with one bright flash.

What very few people know (but you're about to be one of them) is that Fishbone Forest is not a natural forest. By that I mean it was actually planted by a member of the ancient Lyons family many hundreds of years ago (when they weren't quite so ancient) rather than having taken root naturally, like the ancient woodlands to the north.

A grand house, Fishbone Hall, had been built in the middle, surrounded by an equally grand garden with lakes and fountains and terraces and statues, with the forest surrounding that. Over time, people on the outside forgot about the house and garden on the inside and assumed that it was forest through and through. The house and garden were still there in the center but could no longer be described as grand. *Grotesque* might be a better word for them, though somewhat harder to spell.

The ornamental ponds had dried up, their fountains long since silent and still, and the lake was more foul-smelling thick green slime than water. The statues had crumbled, becoming faceless or even headless stone freaks. And the house itself? The house had become so over-grown with ivy, *inside* and out, that it looked more like some giant rock formation than a human-made structure. The whole place had a feeling of decay about it. It seemed unnatural. It seemed that the boundary of human-made and natural had somehow blurred. Some indefinable line had been crossed. There was something *wrong* at the very heart of Fishbone Forest.

Lights shone from many of the glassless windows as Mulch drove up toward the Hall along a slippery path that wound like a great snake through the hideous, bone-like trees.

At last, the path turned into a sweeping driveway and Mulch steered the van through the neglected garden, past crumbling balustrades, ivy-choked statues, and weed-clogged flower beds of long-dead roses. He pulled the English-mustard-colored van to a halt as near to a door at the side of the house as possible. Picking up Fergal's brain in the wrapped jar, he tucked it under his arm, opened the driver's door, and made the short dash from the vehicle to the dryness of the house.

He stood in the bright light of the kitchen, rain dripping from his yellow plastic raincoat and hat.

"Any luck?" asked a bored-looking teenage boy who'd obviously only recently got in from the rain himself and was drying his clothes in front of a roaring open fire. He was wearing an old blue terry-cloth bathrobe.

"Yup." Mulch nodded, putting the brown paper parcel on the kitchen table before proceeding to pull off his coat and hat.

The boy snatched up the parcel and shook it.

"Careful!" pleaded Mulch. "You might damage it!"

The boy was holding the parcel to his ear. "It sounds brainy to me!" he said with a laugh. He liked teasing Mulch, who was so much smaller than he was.

"Toby! Put that down!"

The order was like a whip crack through the air. The stupid grin froze on the boy's face, and he returned the jar to the table.

"Good," said the being who had entered the room. I'd like to be able to call him a man, but that would be stretching the definition a little. There was a lot about him that suggested that he was a male human being—the head, the arms, the legs—but put them all together and you got something altogether *different*.

This frightening apparition was clutching an outsize, roughly stitched teddy bear, which should have made him look, at the very least, *slightly* endearing. In truth, it made him seem all the more strange. The bear was furless—worn with love—and its limbs floppy, but its glass eyes were as shiny and clear as real eyeballs. "You have selected a brain, Mulch?"

"Well, selected might be a bit of an exaggeration,

master," he said. "There was only this one and no others to choose from." Mulch handed him the parcel.

The being—the master—who went by the name of Mr. Maggs, tucked his teddy under one arm and tore off the brown paper to reveal the brain in the jar. He sniffed the air, catching the faintest whiff of pickling vinegar. "It's rather small," he said, and then he caught sight of the label. "This is a child's brain, you fool!"

"It was the only one there!" Mulch protested.

"Then you should have left it and gone back another night!" fumed Mr. Maggs.

"But you said you wanted one tonight!"

"An adult brain. Not a child's!" Mr. Maggs groaned, banging the jar down on the table, Fergal's brain gloop-ing around in the vinegar. Brains in fluid are inclined to gloop.

"I could always go back tomorrow night or the next . . . ," Mulch said defensively.

"You could have if you'd left this brain where it was," snarled Mr. Maggs, "but now that you've stolen this one, every hospital in the city will be on twenty-four-hour brain watch. Buffoon!"

"Nincompoop!" added Toby with a cheeky grin.

Mulch stuck his tongue out at the boy when Mr. Maggs wasn't looking.

Toby picked up the jar. "So what shall I do with this, then, Mr. Maggs? Put it out with the trash?" He was jok-ing, of course. There was no trash collection from this long-forgotten ramshackle house.

"No!" said Mr. Maggs, snatching the brain. "Time is running out. For my little plan to work, Lionel Lyons needs to be alive and well . . . and for him to be alive and well, he must have a brain." He glanced back at the label. "Young Fergal McNally's will have to do. Toby. Go and prepare the operating room."

"Can't I get a drink?" Toby protested.

"GO!" said Mr. Maggs. "But do put some clothes on first!"

CHAPTER TWO

Let's leave Fergal McNally's brain for the time being and pay a visit to the rest of him. You'll find this story doing that kind of thing a lot: switching between the two main theaters of events. I'm not absolutely sure "theaters of events" is quite the right technical term—I didn't go to writing classes—but what I mean by it is straightforward enough. There are two main strands to this exploit: one involving Jackie, Le Fay, Albie, and Josh McNally, and the other involving the people—er, the *beings*—in Fishbone Forest. I don't think I'd be giving too much away by saying that, sooner or later, events collide and these "theaters" become one. (The picture on the cover's a bit of a giveaway on that score, isn't it?) So let's skip forward in time, and to a different location, to drop in on Fergal's funeral.

It was a small affair. At the graveside that wet, wet morning was his father, Captain Rufus McNally, a war hero, and his four surviving children. Their mother, who'd been the one to name Fergal and his siblings—which is an important plot point *so don't you forget it*—had long since died, and for years, Captain Rufus had drunk far too much of what one should really only drink a little of. He'd become a bitter man who spent too much time alone with bottles and his split wooden leg.

Jackie and the others had feared that Fergal's death would bring yet more rage from their father. Instead, it brought his feelings back to him and, after years of his neglecting his children, the McNallys suddenly began to feel like a family again. Fergal's death had also reunited their father with Charlie "Twinkle Toes" Tweedy, who now held an umbrella over his old friend's head in the rain.

Tweedy had been the chief house detective at The Dell Hotel, from which Fergal had fallen to his death. Before that, he'd been a policeman, finishing his career on the force — they wanted to call it the police *service*, but he always saw it as the police *force* — as a very well respected captain, famous for two major character traits. First, he never, ever took a bribe or turned a blind eye to wrongdoing. Second, he danced beautifully whenever he solved a case, which is how he'd earned the name "Twinkle Toes." Before that, he'd fought in the same war that Captain Rufus McNally had, also in the navy . . . and the then young and brave Captain Rufus had saved his life.

The man standing next to Tweedy at the graveside in the rain was called Malcolm Kent. He had come from The Dell with the McNally children to break the news of poor little Fergal's death to their father and had returned for the funeral. Although I describe them as "children," there are two things I should say about Jackie.

Number one, she was old enough to be her brothers' and sister's mother. Number two, she sometimes turned into a jackal. Yup, that's right: a jackal. That may come as a bit of a surprise (especially if you haven't read the First Exploit), but to the McNallys it was no big deal. They were used to it. For as long as they could remember, their big sister had always been able to turn into a jackal, so it never seemed particularly strange or impressive. It was just what Jackie did. But they agreed that it was something they should never discuss with outsiders.

Like most things in life, being able to transmogrify/ metamorph/shape-shift into a howling beast had a downside as well as an upside. Sometimes Jackie couldn't control the change, which could be a little annoying and inconvenient, but it was jolly useful if she needed to be somewhere in a hurry!

But back to the graveside. At this stage, neither Charlie "Twinkle Toes" Tweedy nor Malcolm Kent knew of her secret. Though Malcolm had come from the hotel in the back of the hotel minibus with the McNallys, he didn't work for The Dell. As those of you who are oh-so-lucky enough to have read *The Fall of Fergal* will remember, he worked for Tap 'n' Type (a company that held a typing competition at the hotel, which little Le Fay McNally had just won).

The McNallys were a poor family, and winning the competition was one of the most exciting moments in their lives . . . until Fergal had his appointment with the sidewalk/pavement/ground, and then everything had changed.

The three other people at the graveside were Simon—a friend of Le Fay's in particular—and his parents, Doug and Lenny (which may sound like a man's name, but she was most definitely a woman).

If the McNallys, with their leaky, drafty apartment, were poor, then Simon and his parents were *dirt* poor. They lived in an abandoned greenhouse near the edge of Fishbone Forest. There, it's that place again. They lived there because no one with any sense or money would go within the shadow of the trees.

So there it was: Simon and his parents, Captain Rufus and his children, Twinkle Toes Tweedy and Malcolm Kent. Apart from them, there was just the priest.

In that country, at that time, if you were of that particular branch of that particular faith, the priests sometimes wore a hat that looked rather like a cross between those worn by matadors (bullfighters) and those worn by members of the Mickey Mouse Club (but with less pronounced ears).

If the occasion had been anything other than Fergal's funeral, it's more than likely that the twins, Albie and Josh, would have been nudging each other and giggling at it. Instead, they hardly noticed it and their tears mingled with the drizzling rain. I'm sorry this is so sad, but that's the nature of a funeral, despite the word being an anagram of *real fun*.

The priest spoke a few words over the small, child-size coffin before Twinkle Toes Tweedy and Malcolm Kent gently lowered it into the ground. Fergal's father, Captain Rufus, stepped forward and, scooping a handful of soil from the top of the pile by the grave, tossed it down onto the coffin. It was Jackie's turn next; she stepped forward and—letting out a howl like the jackal she sometimes was—she tossed a single red rose into the hole. She then stepped back and put a supporting arm around her sister, Le Fay. In her hands she clasped a beautiful golden envelope. It had contained a voucher for the prize she'd won in the Tap 'n' Type competition at The Dell Hotel, but now it contained a message for Fergal.

She leaned over the freshly dug grave and dropped the envelope into the hole. It landed on the brass plaque with Fergal's name on it, screwed into the lid of the coffin. Both it and the coffin had been paid for by the hotel management.

Finally, Albie and Josh stepped forward as one. Josh pulled a small rubber ball out of his pocket, and he and Albie held it in their hands together—Albie clasping Josh's right hand with his left. It was their most treasured possession, and I can tell you, they didn't have many possessions, treasured or otherwise. They dropped it into the hole.

It hit the coffin lid, bounced out of the grave, and hit the priest—SMACK!—on the nose.

To her shame, it was Jackie who laughed first, but she was swiftly followed by Albie and Josh *and* Le Fay . . . and soon their father was laughing too. Then Twinkle Toes Tweedy couldn't hold back any longer and burst out into such a silly laugh that he set the others off even more. The suppressed giggles of Simon and his parents soon turned into frantic guffaws.

Malcolm, who was a very nice man, was trying to comfort the priest, whose nose was now bleeding, and only started to laugh when he realized that the priest— the victim of the accident—was shaking with laughter too! Tears of laughter streamed down *all* their faces. They hugged each other. They wiped their tears. They laughed some more. Jackie was now laughing so much her sides hurt. Twinkle Toes Tweedy was bent over double. The priest retrieved the rubber ball from among the floral tributes—flowers, to you and me—and handed it to Josh.

Together he and Albie knelt down and leaned into the grave, dropping the ball on the coffin from a far lesser height so there was less bounce. The laughter subsided and soon the service was over.

As they walked away from the graveside, Rufus McNally couldn't help himself and started laughing again, which triggered yet more hysterics from the others.

"It was the funniest funeral I've ever been to," the priest later told his housekeeper as she put an ice pack on his swollen nose. "They were such nice people."

Back at the McNallys' apartment, which was up a flight of wide concrete stairs, on the second floor from the ground, the mourners gathered for a meager meal of sandwiches and crisps. To the McNallys, it was quite a spread, but they weren't hungry. To Simon and his parents, it was a FEAST. They usually lived off the fruit and veg that fell from the fruit stalls or were thrown to the ground by the stallholders at the daily market in the nearby square. When the market packed up and went home, Simon, his dad, Doug, and his mum, Lenny, moved in, scavenging the discarded boxes. They weren't alone. Other human scavengers were on similar missions.

Lenny became very good at making excellent vegetable stews and vegetable soups, and they ate plenty of fresh fruit. They didn't care about a few splits and bruises, but there wasn't a great deal of *variety*. Bloater paste sandwiches may not be your or my idea of a luxury repast, but Simon and his parents tucked in. As for what some call crisps and others call potato chips, Simon couldn't believe his eyes . . . but felt very guilty at the

loud crunching noises he was making when no one else was eating.

Jackie smiled at him. "Tuck in," she said. "It'd be a terrible waste not to eat it just because *we're* not hungry."

On the table by the window was a photograph of Captain Rufus and Mrs. McNally, proudly holding Fergal as a baby. It was one of only two pictures they had of Fergal. The other hung in "the back room" (which was really at the side). Fergal was wearing a nappy. The weird thing was, he'd been wearing a nappy the day before he died . . . but that had been to disguise him as a baby so that he could travel for nothing on a bus trip! Fate, or someone up there, can play cruel tricks sometimes.

"I wonder what his power was?" said Le Fay in a hushed voice, touching Fergal's face in the photo. "His secret ability?"

"We'll never know now," said Jackie.

By "power" Le Fay meant the thing that made each of them different. Jackie already knew her power, of course.

That was becoming the jackal. Le Fay, Albie, and Josh were yet to discover theirs. They had no idea what they might be. Being almost identical twins, would Albie and Josh have almost identical powers or two totally separate ones? And what about Le Fay?

Somehow their mother had always known what special "power" each of her children would have and had named them accordingly, or so she claimed. Their father, Rufus, had had no say in the matter and had been as surprised as Jackie herself the first time she turned all four-legged and furry and started to howl at the moon.

"The clues are in your names," Mrs. McNally had told her children, but would say no more. "You must find the powers within yourselves!"

Looking at that photo after the funeral, Le Fay wished that Fergal had been named Lazarus; then at least there might have been the chance that he would come back to life somehow. But no such luck — his body was well and truly dead and buried now.

But what Le Fay didn't know about — what *none* of them knew about — was the brain: the one with the faint whiff of pickling vinegar.

CHAPTER THREE

I don't know about you, but despite my warning, all this talk of death, funerals, and wakes has still managed to make me feel a touch on the gloomy side, and I didn't intend to write this — and I doubt that you're reading this — in the hope that we'll all end up feeling thoroughly miserable.

My books are generally thought to be a barrel of laughs, not a barrel of tears . . . not that I've ever *heard* of a barrel of tears and not that I've ever actually seen a barrel of laughs, but people do talk about them. I wonder where the idea came from? Perhaps you could toddle off to your local library and look it up in *The Big Book of Answers.* You can't expect me to do everything for you.

Back already? Good. I hope it was a nice break from all that weeping and wailing and gnashing of teeth. Okay, so we haven't actually had any gnashing of teeth yet, but there's still time *and* it gives me the opportunity to tell you a story about the McNally children's grandmother — Captain Rufus's mum — back in the days when she was still alive. I've heard a different version of this story told about somebody else, but I like the Granny McNally version, so I'm sticking to it. She was an old lady by the time of the incident I'm about to relate and never bothered to wear false teeth, even though all her *real* teeth had long since fallen out.

One day, Granny McNally was sitting in the front pew of her local church, like she did every Sunday, eagerly awaiting the sermon from the nice young preacher with the center part in his hair, when someone she'd never laid eyes on strode into the pulpit and started preaching about Fire and Brimstone and the Horrors of Hell. Now, there's nothing wrong with preaching Fire and Brimstone and the Horrors of Hell if you seriously believe that your fellow human beings are going to end up in Hell unless you do your best to save them. In fact, that would probably be the only right and proper thing to do.

The problem was, the people at the church Granny McNally went to had rather a different idea about religion. *Their* religion had more to do with the nice things people could do to help one another: lending a helping hand and being kind, honest, and true. Devils prodding you with pitchforks in the fiery depths of hell (which they thought of with a small *h* if they thought of it at all) didn't really come into it. Giving shelter to the homeless, food to the hungry, and books to the poor didn't leave much time to worry about much else.

This meant that the congregation at St. James the Lessser (with three *s*'s due to an error by the sign painter over 150 years before) were a bit puzzled and even uncomfortable when this visiting preacher was talking about the truly horrendous things that would happen to them if they didn't "repent" and, thus, ended up in Hell.

"There will be weeping!" cried the preacher, throwing his arms wide. "There will be wailing!" and he made the word *wailing* sound like a long, lamenting wail. "There will be gnashing of teeth!"

Granny McNally put her hand up, like a kid in class.

The visiting preacher was stunned. No one had ever interrupted one of his Fire-and-Brimstone sermons with a question before.

"Yes? What is it?" he spluttered.

"Are you saying I could go to hell?" she asked.

"We could *all* go to Hell!" The preacher nodded fervently.

"And I'll weep and I'll wail and I'll gnash my teeth?"

The preacher nodded. He was certainly getting through to some of these people.

"But what if you don't have any teeth?" she asked, grinning a toothless grin to reveal that her mouth contained her tongue and not much else.

The visiting preacher was staring into a gaping black hole, like the entrance to Hell itself! He began to tremble.

"Teeth," he whimpered, "will be provided."

With that, he fled the pulpit *and* the church and never came back to St. James the Lessser (with three s's) again. The next time the Reverend Norris—the nice young preacher with the center part—was off sick, a different preacher took his place, one who didn't once mention Hell—with or without a capital *H*—and usually stuck to safe topics, such as "being kind to animals" or "a funny thing that happened to me on the way to the church that morning" . . . especially if he saw Granny McNally in the front row, waiting to pounce.

And so, from my favorite Granny McNally anecdote, we return to the younger McNallys and the days immediately following Fergal's funeral. They were some of the hardest they ever had to face and, rest assured, there were still some pretty hard ones to come. With the funeral coming up, Jackie, Le Fay, Albie, and Josh had had something to focus on, an event to get through. Now that it had come and gone, there seemed to be simply nothing more than the-whole-of-the-rest-of-their-lives-without-Fergal to focus on.

Then there was the guilt. When someone dies, there is always guilt: guilt at what one should have said and done but never got around to saying or doing . . . and now it was too late.

Fortunately for us and for the McNallys, events were soon to overtake them, or take them over. Soon there was to be little time for sitting around and feeling sorry for themselves. This was a time for action. It began with Le Fay deciding that she, Jackie, and the twins, Albie and Josh, must go to visit Wandaland. What made her decide? She had no idea at the time, but there were forces at work and all will be revealed. What you can be sure of, though, is it *wasn't* "just one of those things."

So what was this Wandaland that Le Fay was so keen for them to visit that particular rainy day amongst all the other rainy days? It may sound like Wonderland—I'm sure that was intentional—but that's where any similarities cease.

It's hard to imagine anything less wonderful than Wandaland, I can assure you. In the interest of research I've been there, and let me state categorically, whatever the opposite of wonderful is, that's what Wandaland has by the bucket load.

As most of you in a guessing mood will have guessed, Wandaland was named after a person called Wanda. (Or should that be "called after a person named Wanda?" Take your pick.) That person was a very old, large black lady named Wanda de Vere, and she'd built Wandaland all by herself many decades ago. Back then, Wandaland didn't have to compete with TV sets in most houses or computer games and the like. Back then, paint that was now faded or flaking—or faded *and* flaking—was fresh and brightly colored. But even then, it was far from wonderful.

The story goes that Wanda de Vere was descended from slaves. Her grandparents or great-grandparents (there are different versions) had been bought and "belonged" to a white man in a country a long way from their original home, but they had escaped via something called the Underground Railroad—which wasn't really underground and wasn't really a railroad—and ended up settling in the town where the McNallys now lived. It's shocking to think that there was a time and a place where "owning" people was considered to be an okay thing to do. It's easy to be dismissive about something like that because it has "nothing to do with us," but—if I can put on my serious hat for a moment and step outside the action of the story—it's up to us to make sure things like this never happen again.

Now, back to Wanda. When she was twenty-one and still called Wanda Smith, she married a man named Vernon de Vere, who had made a fortune selling safety matches. There was a time when matches were far from safe and they'd rub against each other in your trouser pocket as you walked along—if you wore trousers—and set fire to your leg . . . or they'd rub against each other in someone else's trouser pocket as they walked and set fire to *their* leg. So safety matches were very much in demand when they came along. And come along they did, in wagons (and later, trucks) with DE VERE MATCHES emblazoned on the sides in fiery orange letters.

Wanda and Vern de Vere (as he liked to be called) were very happy together, but, sadly, he was killed in the war. (It doesn't really matter which war; it was simply one of those wars referred to as "the war" once it was over, because it was the freshest war in people's minds until the next, and even more dreadful, one came along.)

To encourage people to enlist—sign up to join the army and fight—recruitment offices were set up in church halls, town halls, and empty shops across the land. Large temporary signs were put up outside these offices with patriotic slogans designed to encourage all right-thinking young(ish) men to sign up, then and there, to fight.

It was one such sign that fell on Vern de Vere's head as he was innocently walking past a temporary recruitment office near one of his factories. I'm led to believe that the wording on it was: REAL MEN DON'T WAIT TO BE ASKED TO FIGHT FOR WHAT'S RIGHT.

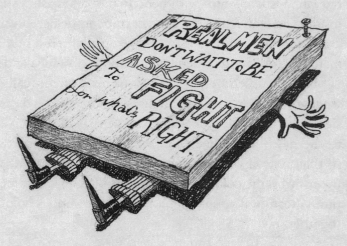

Because Vern de Vere had been a well-known and well-respected businessman and because it was an army sign that had flattened him on the pavement, the government decided to pay Wanda a war widow's pension as a mark of respect.

Following his final wishes to the letter, she had her late husband's coffin made like a giant DE VERE matchbox and cremated (burnt), even though most people preferred to be buried back then. But if matches are your business, you're going to want to be burnt, aren't you?

His ashes were placed in a bronze urn shaped like a giant safety match, especially commissioned and sculpted by the (then) famous artist Hans Gobble (as in the noise turkeys are supposed to make).

Wanda was never quite the same after Vern de Vere died. She took a further turn for the worse when, in the 1950s, Hans Gobble statues became so sought after that her late husband's urn (with her late husband's ashes still inside) was stolen to order for a corrupt art dealer. It was around about then that Wanda gave up all interest in the match factories and turned her attention to Wandaland.

She built an entire high street, or main street (call it what you will), in which the houses that lined it on either side most resembled one-room garden sheds. This was in the days before one could buy self-assembly sheds, so that in itself was quite unusual. Then Wanda painted them in bright colors—and I mean BRIGHT—sometimes creating new shades by mixing the various colors together.

Often when guidebooks talk about a person "building" a place, they mean that the person came up with the idea or designed the plans or just paid for it to be built, but more often than not, they didn't physically build it all themselves (brick by brick, plank by plank, stone by stone). They were simply in charge and put their names to it. Not so with Wanda. Come rain or shine, it was her out there doing the sawing, hammering, or painting, with just her dog for company.

People with opinions (and such people are easy to find) were of the opinion that Mrs. de Vere was creating Wandaland as therapy and the general consensus was—in other words, *most* of these opinionated people agreed—that this was a bad thing. It was good that she was occupying her time with something new but a bad thing that this "thing" was erecting and painting rows of shacks. Shouldn't a rich widow be taking her mind off her husband's death by throwing herself into charitable works, not building some crazy make-believe world?

But like most truly sensible people, Wanda didn't really care what people like that thought. They were welcome to their opinions, and she was welcome to hers. When her self-built shantytown was complete, she got the son of the man who'd come up with the original lettering for DE VERE MATCHES to paint a great big sign that read WELCOME TO WANDALAND. She charged a nominal—very small—entry fee and, in those early days, people flocked to see it. Even most of them who'd tut-tutted came along for a look-see. Everyone wanted to know what Mrs. de Vere had been up to and what was inside those sheds.

Back then, she gave groups guided tours in person. Later, people were left to wander around on their own, and she left handwritten notices pinned up here, there, and everywhere to explain to visitors what was what. Some made sense: *This shed represents a ship on the Sea of Life. The blue at the bottom is the sea. The blue at the top is the sky. One of you step inside while another lifts the lever up and down. This movement represents the waves.*

Other notices were more abstract or (as someone less charitable once put it) "plain weird." These included: *This shed represents the shed-shaped air excluded from this space because the shed itself is taking it up* and *Just because I bothered to write this notice doesn't mean you should bother to read it.* There is the distinct possibility, of course, that Wanda de Vere had a wicked sense of humor!

Wandaland was a very strange place indeed. It wasn't built by a woman with a single vision but one with lots of *different* visions, and most people left very confused. Wanda de Vere seemed to spend most of her time in a little tollbooth by the entrance, taking the money, with a faithful dog curled up at her feet. As the years passed, the nominal fee got more and more nominal until one day, he stopped charging altogether, but by then, few people visited Wandaland anyway . . . but Mrs. de Vere still sat in her tollbooth, meeting and greeting anyone who should pass by.

The dogs changed over the years, though. When one

of her much-loved companions died, she would bury it in her dog cemetery at the far end of the one and only street in Wandaland and then go and choose a puppy from the dogs' home on Dillington Street— Dillington Street Dog Shelter—and this would become her new companion. It would sleep at her feet in the booth for much of each and every day until they went home to her grand apartment in the "no pets" building, where the doorman and concierge politely turned a blind eye.

When Jackie, Le Fay, Albie, and Josh McNally arrived at Wandaland, trying to huddle under one tatty umbrella, Wanda de Vere had been taking her current dog, Nimmo, for a rather wet "walkies" and was just leading him back into the booth on the piece of fraying twine she used as a leash. She smiled at Jackie and the children.

"A warm welcome to Wandaland," she said, which was pretty much what she always said to everyone, rain or shine.

Whereas the sheds had originally been empty—apart from the strange objects and furniture Wanda might have placed in them for aesthetic reasons—nowadays they were sometimes used by carnival folk as places to stage minor entertainments. Instead of pitching a tent, they hung a banner or handwritten sign outside a shed such as PALMS READ, HOT DOGS, CRYSTAL BALL FORTUNE-TELLING, ROASTED CHESTNUTS, TEA LEAVES READ HERE, I GUESS YOUR WEIGHT, YOUR FORTUNE IN THE STARS, and BEARDED FISHES AND OTHER WONDERS. The rows of sheds had become the place of business of the biggest collection of so-called clairvoyants in town.

It was a shrewd move that each fortune-teller had his or her own particular talent. More often than not, a fortune-teller will offer a wide range of services, from tarot card to crystal ball readings. Here in Wandaland, everyone stuck to his or her own speciality, so if you wanted your tea leaves read *and* a palm reading, you had to visit two different sheds with two different fortune-tellers and cross two different palms with silver (in other words, you had to pay them both).

It also encouraged any visitor into fortune-telling to put the fortune-tellers to the test by seeing if each one, with their own method, came up with similar predictions. It was a clever moneymaking enterprise.

"We're here now, so now what?" asked Albie, feeling very cold and very wet.

"What now?" asked Josh.

"Exactly," said Jackie, looking at Le Fay through the steady drizzle.

"I'm not sure," said Le Fay honestly. "It's just that I really felt we should come."

"I wouldn't mind a hot dog," said Albie.

"Or half a hot dog," Josh added hurriedly, seeing the expression on Jackie's face.

"We don't have money to waste on hot dogs." She sighed.

"Or fortune-tellers," admitted Le Fay.

"If we went to all of these, they'd cost a fortune too!" Josh grinned.

"So what shall we do?" asked Albie.

"Let's look at the dog cemetery," Le Fay suggested.

"But that's a sad place," said Albie.

"No, it isn't," said Le Fay, marching off down Wandaland's one and only street, its potholes filled with rainwater. "At least, it shouldn't be. If you were a dog, wouldn't you want to be one that's loved so much that your owner buries your ashes in a special place with a tombstone and everything?"

Jackie caught up with her sister and gripped her hand. "Perhaps it's too early to be visiting a dogs' graveyard after . . . after Fergal's funeral," she whispered.

Le Fay hesitated. Remembering that Jackie sometimes

turned into a jackal—who could forget?—and that jackals come from the dog family, Le Fay wondered whether her big sister would find a dog cemetery an even sadder place than others might. What on Earth had possessed her to insist the others come to this place anyhow? And in the rain?

Then she saw the sign: FREE FORTUNE-TELLING TODAY ONLY. It was over the door of one of the tattiest sheds, once painted in bright green paint that had faded to little more than a greenish tint on the grain, and the door was wide open. "Look!" She pointed.

Seeing the word *free*, Josh and Albie were inside that shed before you could say, "Which twin's which?" Le Fay and Jackie followed.

The inside can be described in two words (or three if you include *and*): *small* and *dark*. It was a tight squeeze, and what little daylight there was filtered through a small window ingrained with years of grime.

They blinked to adjust to the lack of light. At the right-hand end of the shed, steeped in shadow, sat a fortune-teller. The top of his head was swathed in a red turban (which had definitely seen better days), and his nose, mouth, and chin were hidden by a scarf made out of the same material.

You'd probably see people in more impressive costumes at any amateur dramatics production, or at any fancy dress party, or could make a better costume using bits and bobs from any half-decent dressing-up box, but the McNally children—not that Jackie was a child anymore—had neither seen an amateur dramatics production *nor* been to a fancy dress party *nor* had a dressing-up box, so the Fortune Teller looked pretty exotic to them.

All they could see of his face were his eyes.

"Which one of you has come to have their fortune foretold?" asked the Fortune Teller, his voice disappointingly high and quavering.

Jackie pushed Le Fay forward. "It was your idea to come here," she reminded her.

"M-Me," said Le Fay, suddenly feeling nervous. "My name is—"

The Fortune Teller held up a hand to stop her from going any further. The mottled skin looked like old parchment—which is what one looks for in a wise old mystic—but his watchband was made of yellow plastic, and his sleeves were frayed, which somewhat lessened the effect. "Sit," he commanded.

Le Fay sat on a small three-legged stool facing him. The other three crowded behind her. The Fortune Teller took Le Fay's right hand, and the moment they touched, he jolted back, eyes widening, as if he'd been given a nasty burn or an electric shock, but he tightened his grip rather than letting go. "Powerful forces are at work here!" he said in a squeaky voice.

"I'll bet you say that to everyone," Albie whispered. He was clearly unimpressed.

Josh nudged him in the ribs and tried not to giggle.

The Fortune Teller's gaze came to rest upon the almost-identical twins. "The giant killer and the musician, I see," he said, the tone of his voice changing and a look of confusion passing across his face, clearly visible in the only part of it that the others could see: his eyes.

"Huh?" said Albie.

"The name's Josh, not Jack," said his brother, assuming that this fraud had been referring to Jack the Giant-Killer, the hero of a fairy tale that Jackie had told them about when they were younger.

"He should stick to the 'powerful forces' script," Albie muttered.

"Quiet!" said Jackie, who was always very insistent that they be polite. The shed smelled of damp McNallys.

The Fortune Teller's manner had noticeably changed. He turned Le Fay's hand palm up and leaned forward to study it. "Of late you have experienced great joy and great sadness. Though poor in possessions, you are rich in the heart and the love of your family. . . . You . . . you . . ."

He sat bolt upright, the long, flowing scarf falling from his face. His eyes grew wider still and he stared with the look of a blind man.

When he spoke again, they could see his mouth now, but the voice was completely different. It was a woman's voice: "You have buried Fergal but not his brain," it said.

The McNally children gasped as one.

"You have buried Fergal but not his brain!" the voice repeated.

Le Fay pulled her hand away. "What is this? Some kind of joke?" she demanded, her anger overcoming any timid feelings she might have had. "Well, it's not funny."

"Find the boy's brain," said the voice coming from the old man's mouth.

"Wh-wh-where is it?" stammered Jackie, her hand gripping Le Fay's shoulder. "Where can we find it?"

"Fishbone Forest," said the voice. The Fortune Teller toppled backward and hit his head against the shed wall. Le Fay jumped up to help him, knocking over her stool in the process.

"No!" snapped Jackie. "Outside!"

The McNallys tumbled out into the rain. Jackie was holding the closed umbrella but was far too distracted to open it.

"How did that old fraud know Fergal's name?" asked

Josh, clearly shaken by the experience but doing his best not to let it show (and his best wasn't good enough).

It was Jackie who was physically shaking, though. "Mum . . . ," she said.

"What is it, Jacks?" asked Le Fay.

"That was Mum's voice," she said. "We must go to Fishbone Forest. . . . It was Mum who made you make us come here, Le Fay. And it was Mum speaking to us through that man. . . ."

CHAPTER FOUR

Now, I couldn't blame some of you for muttering, "What a jolly book this has turned out to be. NOT!" but I did warn you, remember? Look back at page 3. I wasn't kidding, now, was I? As well as Fergal's funeral, we've had plenty about dogs dying (and a dogs' cemetery), we've had talk of gnashing of teeth in Hell (with a capital *H*), someone being cremated in a giant matchbox after being killed by a falling sign (only to have his remains stolen), and we've even touched, for the briefest of moments, on the horrors of slavery, but — on the surface — few things can be as shocking as the McNallys learning from their long-dead mother that their recently deceased brother's brain wasn't buried along with the rest of him but was somewhere in the creepiest forest around!!!!!! (My editor had better not remove any of those exclamation marks, even though there are six of them. A statement like that needs each and every one of them. Less than half a dozen just won't do.) And where did the McNallys learn this shocking news? Shut in a shed with a fortune-teller. Well, one thing's for sure, you don't get to hear about these kinds of exploits every day.

Jackie, Le Fay, and the twins headed for the exit, umbrella still down. They hurried as one past the handful of other stragglers who'd decided to visit the extraordinarily unwonderful Wandaland on such a gray, wet day.

"Are you sure it was Mum's voice?" asked Le Fay.

"Do you think I could ever forget it?" asked Jackie. Being so much older than the others, she had many more memories of their mother, who had died when Fergal had been born.

"But *how* could she speak to us?" demanded Albie. "I don't believe in ghosts!"

"Shouldn't we stay and talk to that guy?" said Josh, meaning the Fortune Teller. "He might know some more."

"I doubt it," said Albie. "He had you down as Jack the Giant Killer and me as a rock star!"

The twins both gave a halfhearted laugh.

"It *was* Mum and she wants us to save Fergal's brain," said Jackie.

"That still doesn't explain how—"

Jackie stopped in her tracks and snarled, "I think you're forgetting something," and the others came to a standstill beside her. "We're not like other people. We're different. I turn into a jackal and all three of you have special powers too, it's just that we don't know what they are yet. We got those from our mother. How? Because she was special too. Now, I'm not saying that Mum is still

42

alive in some other form in some other place, I'm simply saying that her power lives on *through us*. Maybe that means that in times of real importance, such as NOW, we can hear her speak to us. It's not her in person . . . it's her in essence . . . in spirit . . . and no, I don't mean the spooky white-sheet-ghost-rattling-chains kind of spirit. . . . Do you see what I'm saying?"

The rain pitter-pattered down on their soaking wet hair.

"It's the source of our powers telling us that we must find Fergal's brain?" asked Albie.

"Like it was somehow the power inside me that made me insist we all come here today?" said Le Fay, deep in thought.

"Exactly," said Jackie. "There has to be some reason to it all."

"But how did Fergal's brain end up in Fishbone Forest?" Le Fay shuddered because, unlike you and me, she had no idea about it being put in a jar of pickling vinegar at Sacred Heart Hospital or being stolen by Mulch and taken back to that teddy-bear-hugging being, Mr. Maggs. "That's one of the last places I'd want to go."

"Name a *good* place for a brain hunt," said Josh.

"Good point," said Jackie. They headed for the exit. They passed the tollbooth with Nimmo curled up, out of sight, at Wanda de Vere's feet.

"Have a nice day!" she called after the McNallys as they left Wandaland behind them.

*　　*　　*

Following Mr. Maggs's instructions, Toby was preparing the operating room, deep in the basement of the ruinous Fishbone Hall. If you're imagining something out of a Frankenstein movie, with different-colored chemicals bubbling and smoking inside glass beakers and test tubes, a huge wooden operating table with straps to hold the patient down, and an enormous wall-mounted lever for switching on the electric current, you couldn't be much further from the truth.

This was one of the few rooms in the entire building that was ultramodern and ultraclean, like a high-tech operating room in an expensive private hospital (not that there were many of those in that particular country at that particular time).

Every surface and every surgical instrument was already gleaming, but Toby knew not to argue with his master. He'd been told to prepare the operating room and that included cleaning everything, so cleaning everything he was. He even placed the gleaming surgical instruments—everything from razor-sharp scalpels to metal tongs and tweezers—in a stainless-steel dish, which he lowered into a special sterilizing machine, and whilst they heated up, he washed down the surfaces with disinfectant from a spray bottle.

Toby had a Discman clipped to the waistband of his jeans and was listening to heavy metal as he worked, singing out loud—not that he could hear his own voice too well above the sound of "Death Throws" pumping through the headphones.

"'*Spirits of the dead!*'" he shouted, following the chorus of his favorite song by the band Walking with Skeletons. As you may have guessed by now, Toby was, in many ways, what many people consider "a typical teenager." If you have a teenage brother, you'll know exactly what I mean. He was the kind of guy whose feet would stink in his trainers/sneakers/gym shoes if Mr. Maggs hadn't had such strict rules about everything. And even young Toby wasn't stupid enough to deliberately get on the wrong side of Mr. Maggs.

As he scrubbed and cleaned and sang to himself, he was unaware that the aforementioned Mr. Maggs had entered the room. Mr. Maggs moved surprisingly quietly for such a large being. (I nearly said "man," but for reasons already outlined, you know just how wrong that would have been.) It wasn't simply that he was "light on his feet"—he could have been as noisy as he'd liked in this instance, and Toby still wouldn't have heard him—but he had a way of seeming to melt into place—no, *fade* into place—out of nowhere, but that wasn't possible, was it? It's just that he was very good at being there when one least expected it . . . but it wasn't sudden. There was a sense that he'd somehow been there all the time but one hadn't noticed him until then. Actually, it's very hard to explain, which is why I'm not doing such a great job, but I hope you get the idea: Even Mr. Maggs's entrances and exits were strange.

Toby looked up, and there the master was. "Ready?" Mr. Maggs mouthed, having pulled down the surgical paper mask that had been covering his mouth.

"Ready!" Toby nodded, throwing the cloth he'd been using into a bin lined with a yellow trash bag marked WASTE FOR INCINERATION. He pulled off the disposable gloves he'd been wearing and threw them in too, then clicked off his Discman.

"Excellent," said Mr. Maggs. "Would you be kind enough to have Lionel Lyons join us?"

Toby hurried across the operating room to a large stainless-steel door set into the far wall at waist height. He grasped its handle, and it opened with a hiss to reveal the end of a large drawer. He slid out the drawer, on which lay an elderly gentleman about to suck an orange-flavored ice cream, frozen solid. It wasn't just the ice cream that was frozen solid, but the gentleman too.

"Bother!" muttered Toby under his breath.

"What is it?" demanded Mr. Maggs.

"Er . . . there must be something wrong with the temperature control. He's supposed to have thawed out by now and—"

"Be nicely chilled out and ready for the operation," said Mr. Maggs, striding across the room, his outsize teddy clutched to him. He took one look at Lionel Lyons and groaned. "Am I surrounded by buffoons?"

"I could put him in the microwave," Toby suggested,

hoping beyond hope that Mr. Maggs wouldn't explode into one of his rages.

"How many times have I told you not to call it that?" his master demanded. "It's not a cooker!"

Try telling that to Mulch, Toby thought, thinking back to the many times he'd seen the little man heat his meat pies in the giant thawing machine, but he said nothing.

Toby slid the very frozen Lionel Lyons off the drawer and onto a gurney/trolley/stretcher-on-wheels thingy and wheeled him over to what he and Mulch thought of as the giant microwave (one of Mr. Maggs's own designs). He opened the huge door and slid the frozen man (with frozen ice cream) inside and shut the door.

"Set the heat to slow thaw and the timer to three hours," said Mr. Maggs. "We must damage as little tissue as possible. . . . Yet another delay. Why must I always suffer delays? Where's the brain?"

"I thought you had it," said Toby.

Mr. Maggs hit him with his teddy.

Approximately two and a half hours later, there was a knock at the door of Mr. Maggs's study, which was a strange half-indoor/half-outdoor room, with ivy growing all over one side of the massive oak desk, behind which Mr. Maggs now sat.

He assumed it was Toby come to report that Lionel Lyons had fully thawed. "Enter!" he boomed.

It was, however, Mulch who opened the door and

came through the doorway, with a large package under one arm. This was a matter of courtesy because he could just as easily have stepped through any number of large gaping holes in the various inner walls.

It was still raining hard in that part of the study open to the sky, and the overstuffed chairs were getting soggier and soggier and turning a darker shade of beige.

"What is it?" asked Mr. Maggs, stroking his teddy bear's head between the ears.

"Excellent news, master," said Mulch, with a kind of fawning bow. (That's a bow as in bending your head, not a bow as in something you fire an arrow with or wear in your hair.)

"What is it?"

"An adult brain! We have an adult brain!" said Mulch, barely able to contain his excitement.

Mr. Maggs suddenly seemed even bigger as he leaned forward and asked, "Where? Show me! Show me."

Mulch placed the package on the desk. He took the lid off a plastic box and there, packed in ice, was indeed an adult human brain.

Tears sprang to the master's eyes. "Where did you get it?" he wanted to know.

"It was delivered," Mulch explained. "The card that came with it says: *From a grateful donor, Cousin Ralphie*," he read.

"You can always rely on family." Mr. Maggs sighed happily, looking even more like a grinning pumpkin than Mulch had ever seen.

"So what shall I do with the juvenile's brain?" asked Mulch, relieved to be out of a tight spot and to see his master happy at last.

"I have no use for it now," said Mr. Maggs with the wave of a hand. "Get rid of it."

Oh dear, oh dear, oh dear.

CHAPTER FIVE

"Why don't you want us to tell Dad about Fishbone Forest?" asked Le Fay. "He seems so much better . . . so much *nicer* since Fergal died."

"Yeah," agreed Josh. "Nowadays he doesn't just talk to us when he's telling us to get him something or *not* to do this or *not* to do that."

"Until lately, I'd forgotten he could talk without shouting," added Albie.

It was true. Captain McNally really did seem a different man: a *caring* dad.

"That's as may be," said Jackie, sounding very grown up, because "that's as may be" is the kind of phrase that grown-ups use. "But what do we tell him? That Mum, or the power-of-Mum, spoke to us through some pretend fortune-teller at Wandaland and told us that Fergal's brain isn't buried with the rest of him but is somewhere in Fishbone Forest?"

"I know it sounds crazy, but so does you turning into a jackal . . . and he's used to that. He knows that we all have special powers, and *that's* because Mum used to have them too, so why shouldn't he believe us?" Le Fay reasoned.

It was still raining, but they'd wanted to talk away from the apartment, so they were up a tree in the local park. To call it a park was a bit grand, truth be told, though it appeared on maps as GARLAND PARK. There were no flowers or anything. It was more a large patch of grass, with a single tree right in the center. Near the tree was a large hole (about the size of an Olympic swimming pool), which had opened up without warning a month before. It was now roped off to discourage people from falling into it. This was just one of a series of holes that had started appearing right across the country eighteen months or so previously. No one seemed to know what had caused this outbreak (or breakout) of holes, and no one seemed to know how to stop them. Some experts thought that their cause was geological; some thought that their cause was supernatural; others were convinced that they were created by extraterrestrials. Most people simply got used to them, in the same way that people get used to living with volcanoes or earthquakes or bombing from enemy planes. The holes were okay so long as you, your family, your friends, or your home didn't fall into one.

Years ago, some kids had put a sheet of corrugated iron in the top branches of the tree to act as a kind of roof, and the McNallys (and others) often used the tree in Garland Park as a sort of floorless tree house, sitting or standing on the branches. If you couldn't afford to hang out in one of the cafés or burger places, where you had to buy something to sit there, you could literally hang out of the tree.

Now Albie and Josh were standing in the highest branches, directly above the seated Le Fay and Jackie (who felt that she was far too old to be climbing trees and that it was undignified for a part-time member of the dog family, what with being a jackal and all, when it was *cats* that were natural tree climbers).

"We could ask Mr. Tweedy for help," Albie suggested. "What with him being a detective and all."

"I can't see the point in going after the brain anyway," said Josh, his voice little more than a whisper.

"What?" demanded Jackie.

"Nothing," said Josh guiltily.

"No, go on," said Jackie. "We must all have our say."

"Well, even if we do find Fergal's brain, it's not going to bring him back, is it?"

"That's true," said Jackie, "but don't you think it should be buried with the rest of him?"

"Fergal won't miss it," said Albie, coming to his twin's defense.

"That's also true, but it's important to Mum—"

"Or the power-of-Mum," Le Fay interrupted.

"—that we find it, and that ought to be reason enough. Shall we take a vote?" asked Jackie.

"There's no need," said Josh. "Of course we're all in this together. I was only thinking out loud, that's all."

"Then tomorrow, it's Fishbone Forest, here we come!" said Le Fay, raising her voice to be heard above the rain beating down on the corrugated iron. Despite the effort, she didn't sound very enthusiastic.

When Lionel Lyons had finally thawed out, Mr. Maggs set to work placing the brain so kindly donated by Mr. Maggs's Cousin Ralphie inside his skull, connecting all the relevant bits here and there. (That may sound a bit wishy-washy and lacking in medical terms, but I've left it this vague for three reasons. Firstly, because to the lay— that means "nonexpert"— reader, none of these technical terms will mean a great deal; secondly, if I say much more than "he peeled back the skin off the top of the head, sawed off the top skull, removed the damaged brain, putting the donated one in its place, connected it all up, then put the head back together again," it's bound to put some of you off your breakfast, lunch, tea, or supper; and thirdly, if I put in too much detail, it might encourage the odd reader—and I mean *odd*—to try out a little DIY brain surgery him- (or her-) self . . . and my name could come up in the court case, with the defense lawyer stating, "My client used Philip Ardagh's *Heir of Mystery* as an instruction manual during the brain surgery; therefore it must be Mr. Ardagh's, and not my client's, fault that the patient died." See what I mean?)

Suffice it to say that it was an extremely long and complicated operation and, requiring both hands, meant that Mr. Maggs's teddy had to be tied to his waist with the cord of his operating gown.

Toby, meanwhile, acted as his nurse, handing him all

the relevant surgical implements, swabs, bandages, and the like, but Mulch was banished to the other side of the glass. He had assisted the master in earlier practice attempts at what he called "reanimation" but had been a little clumsy on more than one occasion, which had thrown Mr. Maggs into a violent rage. Fortunately, Mr. Maggs had been violent toward various items of furniture in the room rather than toward Mulch in person, but the damage was done. This was why Mulch was now given the supposedly more simple tasks, such as breaking into Sacred Heart Hospital to steal a brain. And look how displeased Mr. Maggs had been with the result of *that*.

Watching Mr. Maggs now as he glued the sawed-off top of the skull back in place and pulled the skin back down into position and nimbly sewed a line of stitches, Mulch thought how unfair it was that Toby was the one in there with him. Mulch had worked for the master for years, but Toby was just a kid and he got to be taking part in one of Mr. Maggs's most dramatic projects yet . . . for not only was the surgery itself so remarkable, but having a version of Lionel Lyons up and about was of vital importance too. This man was crucial to Mr. Maggs's future. The master had plans and these plans required massive funding, funding that L. Lyons, Esquire, could supply.

Mulch stared through the glass, wishing that there was some way to prove his worth to Mr. Maggs. He so wanted his respect.

The operation complete, Lionel-Lyons-with-someone-else's-brain (or should that be someone-else's-brain-with-Lionel-Lyons's-body because, after all, it's the brain that does the thinking and it's the thinking part of you that *mostly* makes you who you are) was wheeled into the "recuperation room" just off the operating room and wired up to a number of monitors that would set off various alarms around the crumbling Fishbone Hall should the patient's "vital signs"—whatever they might be—become dangerously abnormal.

Exhausted from his work, Mr. Maggs and his teddy went for a sleep in the enormous four-poster bed in his bedroom, or "bedchamber" as he preferred to call it. Like the desk in his study, much of this massive bed was overgrown with ivy. It was fortunate that the bed had a canopy because, again like his study, part of the room was open to the elements and the rain came pouring in.

Mr. Maggs lay on his back, staring up at the canopy, his teddy clasped to his chest, face up. Despite his tiredness he couldn't sleep; there was such a mixture of excitement, triumph, and the fear that things might still not succeed. If this reanimation worked . . . if he could pass off the once-dead Lionel Lyons as an alive and kicking "I've-never-felt-so-good" Lionel Lyons, then phase II of his plan could come into effect. He would be able to implement his *Manifesto of Change* . . . and the world wouldn't know what had hit it.

As his master lay in his bed, thinking of the future, Mulch struggled on with his raincoat and dashed out to his van the color of English mustard. He pulled out the choke, put his foot on the clutch, and turned the key in the ignition. The engine was cold and wet, and it took a number of false starts before the little van's engine spluttered to life. He released the hand brake and the car lurched forward.

No sooner had he started off down the drive than the rain seemed to get much worse. The windshield wipers were fighting a losing battle and Mulch could see next to nothing. He wasn't too bothered, just so long as he could stay on the path that led to one of the gates out of there. It wasn't as if this was a public road and he was in danger of hitting another vehicle or human being. There were no other people crazy enough to set foot in Fishbone Forest except for Mr. Maggs and Toby. No, scratch that. That should, of course, just be Toby. Mr. Maggs didn't quite meet all the criteria to fit in the "people" category.

Wanda de Vere was upset, to say the least. Bumbo had gone missing. Bumbo may seem a slightly strange name for a dog—even a bumbling one—but, as anyone who takes the time to read the dogs' names carved on the tombstones in Wandaland's dog cemetery will know, for some reason, Wanda gave all her dogs names ending in the letter o. You may recall that, for example, the dog Wanda had with her at the ticket booth back on page 33 was called Nimmo. In fact, Nimmo was a replacement for Bumbo, who has only just gone missing in this strand of the story. In other words, he came *after* Bumbo in the whole scheme of things but got mentioned *before* him. How and why? Remind me to explain it all a little later on.

When Wanda spoke to the doorman and concierge at her building, they assured her that they hadn't seen the dog slip out on its own, and they were both sure that at least one of them would have noticed because the hallway was never left unattended.

"But what if your back was turned and he slipped out behind another tenant who'd opened the door for himself?" she asked the concierge.

"I've worked here for seventeen years, Mrs. de Vere," he said respectfully, "and in all that time, I've only ever seen one person open the door for him- or herself, and that's you."

Wanda lived in a very expensive apartment block occupied by very rich people who weren't used to doing things for themselves. The richest people in the country generally had homes in the capital (where The Dell Hotel was, from which Fergal fell from the window), but quite a few lived in the McNallys' hometown. This was because it was once a busy river port and many families had made their fortunes from shipping and import and export in the eighteenth and nineteenth centuries.

People from such families, such as those in Wanda de Vere's building, had cooks to cook for them, housekeepers to keep house for them, and butlers to butler or buttle for them (both terms are correct and I, personally, prefer "buttle," not that I have a butler), along with a whole host of general servants to generally serve them. Some of them even had people to help them dress in the morning. About the only thing they did all on their own, in addition to going to the toilet, of course, was to blow their own noses. The reason for this was because, no matter how rich and lazy you are, you don't want to be reminded of the time your mum took a hanky out of her handbag and, in front of all your friends when you were trying to act cool, pressed it up against your nose and said "blow." Wanda had to admit that she couldn't imagine any of them actually *opening the door* for themselves.

"But what about the tradespersons' entrance?" she asked the doorman. That was the entrance and exit at the back of the building, used by anyone who wasn't actually a tenant or accompanying a tenant. (In other words, your butler could use the front entrance if he was with you but not on his own.) There was no doorman or concierge there, just a security guard ready to sign for packages delivered by post/mail/courier and to make sure no "undesirable" came in to shelter from the rain, or to find some shade, or to be a general nuisance or steal something. People were coming in and out of those doors all the time.

"If your dog somehow got out of your apartment and down to the ground floor, Mrs. de Vere, then there is the possibility that it got out of the tradespeople's entrance, I grant you," he said. "But I'm sure someone would have noticed. This is a no-pets building. A dog on the loose would be something out of the ordinary. Everybody would notice."

The concierge then checked with the security guard sitting behind a small desk at the tradespersons' entrance. "Sure, I saw a dog," said the security guard. His name was Jimmy Spleen, and it was his first week on the job. The usual security guard was off sick. "I don't know how it got in here in the first place, but I had it out of that door and out on the street before anyone could shout blue murder."

He saw the look of horror on the concierge's face.

"I know how strict they are about the no-pets rule here," he added. "Did I do something wrong?"

"No, Jimmy," sighed Mrs. de Vere kindly. "It wasn't your fault."

Mulch took the corner too fast in the wet, and the little van slid across the track in a spray of mud. Steering into the skid and then out again, he kept in control of the vehicle and out of the trees and was feeling relieved . . . until seconds later, he hit something with a terrible THUD.

Mulch stopped the van and clambered out into the pouring rain and looked back down the track. He could make out a mound of wet fur in the roadway. He hurried back to it.

He'd knocked down a dog.

Mulch let out a groan of despair. He loved animals. He carefully lifted up the whimpering dog in his arms and carried him to the van. Laying the injured animal on the passenger seat, he found a place to turn the van around and headed back to the crumbling mansion as fast as he dared drive in the wet.

CHAPTER SIX

"Can you sit up?" Mr. Maggs asked "the patient," as he chose to call Lionel Lyons's body with the new brain.

The patient opened his eyes and stared up at the strange-looking being who'd performed the operation. He smiled. *"Bonjour, mes amis, comment ça va?"* he said, his voice croaky (no doubt as a result of his vocal cords being frozen and unused for some time).

"It worked, master!" Toby whooped with delight. "You're a genius!" He did a little victory lap around the bed in the recuperation room. It wasn't up to Twinkle Toes Tweedy's standards, but it was nice to see nonetheless. "This is incredible. . . . I'm a part of history in the making."

Mr. Maggs gave Toby one of his dagger-in-the-eyes stares. "Did you ever doubt me?" he demanded.

"N-N-No, of course not, Mr. Maggs," said Toby. "You're the man! The . . . er . . . ." He couldn't come up with the right word so quickly switched to: "You're amazing!"

"This is just the beginning," Mr. Maggs whispered, almost glowing with obvious pride. "But what's he saying?"

"*Je m'appelle Jean. Est-ce que vous voulez sortir avec moi?*" The patient looked around.

"The man is babbling like an idiot!" Mr. Maggs roared. The fleeting sense of achievement had quickly turned to rage and incomprehension. "And will you stand still?"

"Sorry," said Toby, stopping in his tracks. "But it's early days, master, and you've achieved the impossible. The successful reanimation of a human being. . . . Genius, Mr. Maggs! Genius!"

"*Ma mère n'est pas à la maison . . . ,*" said the patient, still smiling but looking less sure of himself now.

"What's he saying?" Mr. Maggs demanded.

"How should I know?" asked Toby, leaning over the patient. "I think he might be French."

"WHAT???" bellowed Mr. Maggs.

"You know, French. From France."

"I know what French is, you fool," said Mr. Maggs. "But *why?*"

"Don't look at me, master," said a more nervous Toby. "Mulch said your Cousin Ralphie sent you his brain. Was your cousin French?"

"It wasn't his *own* brain, you idiot! It was a brain my Cousin Ralphie had . . . had *acquired.* But why would he provide me with a French brain?"

"How should I know?" Toby said once again, this time with an actual shrug. "Can you tell the nationality of a brain just by looking at it?"

Mr. Maggs pushed the teenager to one side and leaned right over the patient. "C-a-n y-o-u s-p-e-a-k

E-n-g-l-i-s-h?" he asked very slowly and clearly, as though talking to an idiot.

"*Je crois vous ne m'avez pas rendu juste.*" The patient frowned. He sat up suddenly—almost hitting Mr. Maggs's head with his own—and swung his legs over the edge of the bed. Then he seemed to notice his hands for the first time and held them up, as if to study them, with a mixture of surprise and fascination. "*Plume de ma tante!*" he gasped.

"His coordination seems excellent!" said Toby, clearly impressed by the way the patient had sat up and swiveled so abruptly. Mr. Maggs had instructed him to make observations of the man's behavior.

"Great," said Mr. Maggs, as though "great" was the last thing he was feeling. "I have a well-coordinated patient who has to pretend to be Lionel Lyons in the next few days, and he doesn't even understand English! Marvelous!" He punched the pillow on the bed. A single feather fluttered free. "Wonderful!" He made that last word sound about as wonderful as Wandaland.

"Perhaps it's the medication you gave him? The drugs?" Toby suggested doubtfully. "You said that they, as well as the operation itself, might cause confusion, lack of coordination, and depression even. . . ." Soothing the master was an important role in his duties around Fishbone Hall. Being around an unhappy Mr. Maggs was not a pleasant experience.

"Why would the drugs make him speak French, you BUFFOON?" wailed Mr. Maggs. "Do you think they were made in France? Do you think that could have made any difference?"

Toby was about to say "How should I know?" for the third time when he thought better of it. "You're the genius, Mr. Maggs, not me," he pointed out.

Mr. Maggs clutched his teddy bear to him and gave him an extra-loving squeeze. "I don't need to be reminded of that," he said.

The patient stood up, took two unsteady paces, and then fell to the floor on his back, his legs still "walking" in midair. "No sniggering at the back!" he snapped. "And open your textbooks to page twenty-two."

Mr. Maggs looked at Toby and Toby looked at Mr. Maggs. They both smiled as realization dawned.

"Start translating from line eight, Jones," said the patient, still pumping his legs back and forth, "beginning with *Madame Mustard est malade.*"

"He's not French!" said Toby.

"He's a French *teacher,*" said Mr. Maggs and Toby together.

Things were looking up.

Now it's time to take a short pause to take stock of what exactly happened when as this latest Unlikely Exploit unfolded, because I don't want anyone getting confused and then blaming me, especially when the McNallys and the occupants of Fishbone Hall are about to meet.

Stefan Multachan—Mulch to you and me—stole the Fergal-brain-in-a-jar and arrived at Fishbone Forest on the day that Fergal died, with the reanimation of Lionel Lyons's body and the French teacher's brain happening soon after . . .

. . . but much of what the McNallys have been up to didn't happen until after Fergal's funeral, a week or so later, in fact. So now that we're getting close to the part where Jackie, Albie, Josh, and Le Fay finally come face-to-face with Mr. Maggs, Toby, and Mulch, don't forget that a good number of days must have passed since the patient sat up and started babbling away in French. It doesn't help that it rained nonstop throughout this story, so it's hard to tell one dull wet day from another.

Now, I'm fully aware that you could have worked this out for yourselves, and some of you probably already have, without really even thinking about it, but I want to make things nice and straightforward for you. There's no need to thank me. It's what I'm here for.

The walk from the McNally house to the North Gate of Fishbone Forest wasn't a short one at the best of times but in the pouring rain seemed to take forever. It would have taken about an hour on the bus, but there was no way the McNallys could afford the fares. Instead they went by what their family called "Shank's pony," which is another way of saying "their own two feet." It's interesting how you can make the most mundane thing sound more interesting just by giving it a different name. Simon's parents, Doug and Lenny, called water "Adam's Ale" (it being about the only thing they ever drank, apart from juice squeezed from old fruit), which made it sound extra cool and refreshing.

Living as they did in an old greenhouse, they got their Adam's Ale from a collection of old oil drums. When the torrential rain started, they were glad because it meant that they'd be sure of a good supply later in the year, when there might be no rain at all. After a week, though, with all the water drums full and the greenhouse beginning to spring leaks in yet more places, like everyone else, they wished that it would stop.

The greenhouse was near the North Gate of Fishbone Forest, and it was here that Jackie, Le Fay, and the twins were heading.

Wet and tired from their walk, they finally made it. Le Fay knocked on the door, which had soggy bits of wood and cardboard filling the frames where panes of glass had long since been broken and gone.

It was Simon who opened it. He was alone.

"Hi," he said, clearly pleased and surprised. "Come on in out of the wet."

He and his parents had obviously done the best they could to make the old greenhouse into a home, using things they'd found—many of which other people had thrown away—or, on rare occasions, had been given.

The greenhouse had been divided into various different "rooms" with "walls" made from strung-up blankets and curtains and, in one instance, from the wood of old fruit crates from the market nailed to a frame.

There were shelves made from proper planks of wood, separated by bricks, one on top of the other, and a table made from a giant reel that had once had telegraph wire coiled around it, lying on its side. There were two old wooden chairs and an old armchair that Simon's mum, Lenny, had found in a Dumpster the previous summer and had dragged all the way across town.

"It's very cozy here," said Jackie politely once they'd taken off their coats. Simon insisted that she sit in the armchair because she was the grown-up. She'd never been to his home before because he'd been more a friend of Le Fay's and Fergal's.

"I could make a fire to dry you off if you like," said Simon. His father had made a wood-burning stove out of an old oil drum, which he'd cut a door into (so they could put wood inside), with a length of metal drainpipe as a chimney (disappearing through a hole in the greenhouse roof).

Jackie knew how precious fuel must be and was quick to say "No, thank you."

"We'll be going out again soon," she added. "We need your help."

"Sure." Simon grinned. "What with?"

"We want to get into the forest," said Le Fay.

The corners of Simon's mouth dropped so quickly, you'd never have guessed that a smile had been there in the first place. "I'm not going in there," he said.

"We're not asking you to," said Albie.

"*We're* the ones who have to get in," said Josh.

"You guys are crazy," said Simon. "No one goes into the forest."

"Are you telling me that you've never been inside? Not even just a few feet to collect firewood?" asked Le Fay. "It'd be a great place to collect wood, and it's right on your doorstep."

Simon shook his head. "No way," he said.

Everyone in the town had tales to tell about Fishbone Forest, and the nearer people lived to the place, the more people seemed to be frightened of it. These ranged from stories about hearing strange cries at night or seeing strange colored lights in the sky above it to the tale of a group of teenagers who'd been foolish enough to climb over the railings for a dare and only two or three of them were ever seen again, found wandering the streets foaming at the mouth and ranting like madmen. The story went that these "survivors" were hidden away in some lunatic asylum somewhere and that the authorities had tried to hush the whole thing up.

One story that definitely was true was that a man had once tried to set fire to the forest by tossing a can of gasoline, with a flaming rag in the end, over the railings. The fire was mysteriously put out, and two nights later, the man's own house was burnt to the ground. Fortunately, he hadn't been in it at the time. He moved to a different area. (The "putting out" had been up to Mulch. The revenge fire had been one of the jobs Mr. Maggs had entrusted to Toby because he'd been worried that Mulch would mess it up. The instructions had been to "teach the man a lesson . . . but no injuries." How charmingly considerate.)

Jackie looked straight at Simon. "You have been inside, though, haven't you?" she said. "We're definitely going in, with or without your help, but if you can tell us how to get in without us having to climb up and over the railings, we'd really appreciate it."

"It'd save us slipping in the wet and stabbing ourselves on one of the spikes," said Josh.

"Impaling," said Le Fay. "That's what people do on spiked railings; they get impaled."

"Like Vlad the Impaler, who deliberately spiked people—" said Josh.

"I get the picture," said Simon. "But why do you have to get into the forest?"

"We—" began Albie.

"—can't—" said Josh.

"—tell you—" added Le Fay.

"—that," finished Jackie. "It's family business, Simon. You understand."

"Very important, but very private," said Le Fay.

"I understand," said Simon. Sometimes it's best not to ask such things. "There's a break in the railings where a truck hit them a few years back. Only it's small and low down, so you'll have to crawl through," he explained. "The others should fit through no problem, but you might be a bit too big," he told Jackie.

"Don't worry about me," said Jackie. "I'll find a way."

"Have you been through the gap?" asked Le Fay.

"Only once," said Simon, "and don't you dare ever tell Mum or Dad."

"We won't," Le Fay promised.

"I heard what sounded like an animal in pain—a badger or something—and crawled inside to see if I could find it and help it. . . . I was only in there a few minutes but found nothing but trees. It was scary."

"I'll bet," said Jackie. "Will you tell us where this gap is?"

"I'll show you," said Simon.

"We need to go now," said Le Fay.

"Then let's go," said Simon. He disappeared behind one of the curtain walls and reappeared wearing a home-made cape around his neck, made from an old piece of tarp. His mum, Lenny, had made it for him to keep the rain off.

Le Fay picked up the duffel bag she'd put at her feet. "I almost forgot," she said. "We meant to give you these after the funeral." She opened the bag and pulled out a few clothes, including a raincoat. "They were Fergal's," she said.

To most of us, these clothes would probably have seemed too worn and tatty to give to a charity shop or to a garage sale, but these had been some of Fergal's best clothes (not that he'd been the first to wear them by any means) and they were far better than anything Simon was wearing.

Simon accepted the pile and put them on the table before holding up the raincoat. "Are you sure you don't want them?" he asked.

"Fergal doesn't need them anymore," said Le Fay.

"No . . . ," said Simon. "I suppose not." He took off his tarp cape and put on Fergal's raincoat. "I've never had a coat before," he said. He did up the belt. "Thank you," he said. He couldn't have been happier if someone had given him a brand-new one with a designer label and a buckle made of solid gold. "Thank you very much."

He gave Le Fay a hug.

Le Fay never considered the McNallys to be poor because she considered Simon and *his* family to be poor. Little did she know that Simon didn't consider himself to be badly off either because he had two parents who loved him and *he* knew people who didn't even have a roof over their heads.

It's at times like these I like to remind myself how lucky I am. I think I'll just nip downstairs and tell the cats how much I love them.

(I'm back. I met my wife on the stairs, so I thought I might as well tell her how much I love her too. Now, where exactly was I?)

Simon and the McNally children set off in the rain and followed the railings around the edge of the forest until Simon came to a stop.

"Here," he said, crouching down and parting the branches of a bush growing through the railings at waist level. He revealed a spot where, sure enough, the railings had buckled, making a gap wide enough for all of them but Jackie in her current form to fit through.

"Thanks," said Le Fay.

"How are you going to find your way back once you've done whatever it is you have to do?" asked Simon, watching the raindrops being repelled by the waterproof material of his new (to him) raincoat.

"We've thought of that," said Albie.

"It was our idea," said Josh.

"Together," said Albie.

"We got it from a book full of myths and legends. It had lots of weird stuff in it," said Josh.

"Like people hiding in a large hollow wooden—"

"Cow called Marjorie?" asked Simon, who'd once found a discarded paperback book with a weird hollow cow in it.

"Horse," said Albie. "A large hollow wooden horse."

"The Trojan horse," said Josh. "Full of Trojan soldiers."

"Greek soldiers, actually," said Le Fay.

"And there was a story about a beast named the Minotaur who was half man—" began Albie.

"—and half bull," said Josh.

"He lived in a big maze—"

"—called the labyrinth."

"Get to the point, boys," Jackie insisted. "There's a job to be done."

Albie and Josh combined glares to give her one big one. "In the legend, the hero finds his way to the middle of the maze, where the beast is, with a magic ball of string that unrolls in front of him, leading him straight to the creature's lair. Then he follows the unwound string back through the maze to the entrance and escapes."

Josh put his hand in the duffel bag and pulled out the biggest ball of string Simon had ever seen. It wasn't made up of one long piece but of lots of different pieces of different lengths, thicknesses, and colors—from fat, brown, hairy, and made from hemp to thin, blue, smooth, and made from nylon— all knotted together.

The McNallys had been collecting string for years. You never know when such things might come in handy. Like then, for example.

"This will help us find our way back here—" said Albie.

"—if we tie one end to the railings and unravel it as we go," said Le Fay, getting a word in before Josh had a chance to finish his twin's sentence for him.

The rain was getting even harder now. "It really is time we went in there," said Jackie.

Simon was eyeing the small break in the railings. "I still can't see how you're going to get through, Jackie," he said.

"Don't worry about me," Jackie grinned. "I'm quite a contortionist. Now, you'd better head back home and leave us to it."

Le Fay gave Simon a hug. The twins said thanks.

"Thanks again for the raincoat," said Simon, turning to go. He paused. He looked as though he was torn between a reluctance to leave the McNallys to their secret mission and a desire to put a significant distance between himself and Fishbone Forest.

"Go!" said Jackie.

He went.

When he was gone, Jackie looked around to make sure no one else was watching and then quickly turned into a jackal. Even if you've seen that kind of thing in movies and on TV, done with computer special effects, it's nothing like seeing it happen in real life: the skeleton beneath the flesh changing shape and the smooth human skin turning into a hairy jackal's pelt.

There was the funny side too. Because she was in a potentially public place, Jackie had kept her clothes on during her transformation . . . and human clothes don't fit a jackal too well! Le Fay and the twins quickly pulled them off her once she'd transformed and stuffed them in the duffel bag.

Now all four McNallys were ready to slip into Fishbone Forest in the search for Fergal's brain.

CHAPTER SEVEN

I want you to put yourselves in the McNallys' shoes for
a moment. Not literally, of course, particularly when
Jackie wasn't wearing any on her four paws. (Her shoes
were in the duffel bag, left by the railing with the string
tied to it, marking their exit.) No, what I mean is that
I want you to imagine yourselves in Jackie, Le Fay, Albie,
and Josh's position. They've just snuck inside Fishbone
Forest in search of a missing brain, not knowing what
might lie ahead . . . and after making their way through
the trees for a while, with not even the slightest hint of
what lay around the next corner, do you know what
they saw?

Go on. Guess.

No, seriously. Have a guess.

Fishbone Hall?

No.

The ivy-choked statues and slimy green pond?

No. Have another guess.

Mr. Maggs and his big teddy?

No.

Jackie, Le Fay, Joshua, and Albion had gone in search of a missing brain, and there, standing on the path in front of them, stood a small man WITH A BRAIN IN A JAR.

It felt like going on a treasure hunt on a desert island and finding the treasure not half an hour from the shore: not much of an adventure, but fantastic news if it's a chest full of gold coins you're after rather than hours of action-packed excitement.

The McNallys eyed Mulch through the pouring rain. Mulch eyed the McNallys. It's hard to say who was more surprised.

No one ever dared venture into Fishbone Forest, yet here were three children—two of whom looked almost identical—and the weirdest dog Mulch had ever seen (having never seen a jackal).

A dog! That was it. A thought flashed through Mulch's mind. These children must be looking for the dog that had strayed into the forest a week or so previously. The one he'd knocked down. Poor mutt . . . poor kids. Only a hunt for a missing pet would make anyone in their right mind venture within the walls of this dreadful forest. And even then they'd have to be terribly brave or terribly stupid. He must get them out of the forest before Mr. Maggs caught sight of them.

Jackie, Le Fay, Josh, and Albie, meanwhile, were still recovering from the shock of coming face-to-face with what they took to be Fergal's brain in a jar. Of course it must be Fergal's brain, they reasoned. They were told by powerful forces that Fergal's brain was in the forest, so who else's was it likely to be? The place was unlikely to be full of people casually wandering around in the rain with stolen brains, now, wasn't it?

"GIVE THAT HERE!" said Le Fay, recovering from the shock and launching herself at the strange little man. Mulch pulled back, hugging the jar to his chest. Le Fay landed facedown in a muddy puddle with an "ooof!" She'd winded herself, and the gritty soil stung her hands.

The kids wouldn't have bothered Mulch that much if it wasn't for that mangy dog they had with them. He looked at Jackie—although, of course, he didn't *know* that's who he was looking at—who was baring her teeth at him with an impressive snarl.

"Clear off!" he snapped. "Didn't your mummy and daddy warn you about this place? Fishbone Forest is no place for children."

"You have something that doesn't belong to you—" began Josh.

"—and we want it back," said Albie.

I was right, thought Mulch. They've come for that dog I ran over.

"I won't tell you again," said Mulch. "Every second you're in here, you're in danger. Now get out of it, for your own good."

Jackie sank her teeth into the bottom of Mulch's trouser leg. Mulch almost dropped the jar, and everyone—

including the hairy beast by his foot—held his or her breath as he fumbled to regain his grip. The lid rattled, the brain glooped, and there was the faintest whiff of pickling vinegar.

Jackie let go of his trouser leg.

"Now look what you nearly made me go and do!" Mulch whined. "Control that beast."

"Here, Jacks!" said Le Fay innocently, in a little-girl-calling-her-pet-dog voice. Her big sister played her part and bounded over to her side but then quickly turned and fixed her jackal stare on the man with the brain. Le Fay was covered in mud from her fall. They all looked wet, but she looked wet *and* dirty.

Mulch decided to try another approach. "Listen, kids," he said, his tone more friendly. "My boss is around here someplace and if he catches you here, he'll be angry . . . and I guarantee that if you knew him like I know him, you wouldn't want to make him angry."

"Fine," said Le Fay, bravely stepping forward. "Then give us the brain and we'll go."

Mulch hadn't been expecting this. "The *brain?*" he said. "What do you want with a brain?"

"More to the point—" said Josh.

"—what do *you* want with a brain?" demanded Albie.

For some reason, Mulch looked flustered, guilty. "I . . . er . . . that's none of your business," he said.

Le Fay stepped forward, Jackie the jackal trotting alongside her on padded paws. "Give us the brain and we'll go," she repeated.

"I've had enough of this!" snapped Mulch.

The strange-looking dog—or was it a wolf or something? Mulch wondered—snarled.

Mulch made a decision. He didn't have time to argue, and he didn't like the look of the kids' four-legged friend, whatever it was. He turned and ran.

Jackie and the twins set off in hot pursuit. Le Fay tried running but gasped at a pain in her side. She must have hurt a rib or two when she fell. Albie turned to see if she was all right.

"I'm okay!" she shouted. "Go after him!"

Baaaaaaaad move.

With the others disappearing between the hideous leafless trees, Le Fay now found herself alone in the forest.

Le Fay had always been more sensible than the twins. Rather than get lost, she would make her way straight back to the gap in the railings and wait there. After all, they might need to make a very speedy exit.

Whether the others caught up with the little man and managed to save the brain or not, they'd eventually find their way back to the exit, string or no string to guide them. Jackie had the senses of a jackal. Even if they split up, Jackie was familiar with their scent and would be able not only to sniff them out and round them all up but also to pick up the trail of their scent all the way back to where they'd gotten in. If it wasn't for the rain, that is. Rain could wash away the scent, and then where would they be? The string was an important backup.

Le Fay hurried back down the path, dodging the

bigger puddles, looking for the spot where she'd dropped the ball of string. Her ribs were really beginning to hurt now. She found the ball at the edge of a particularly deep puddle. Head down, she began to follow the already unwound pieces of knotted string that would lead her back to the exit.

"You're far from home, little one," said a voice in the gloom.

Le Fay looked up and gasped at the most extraordinary apparition standing before her.

There was a flash of sheet lightning and, silhouetted against the trees, stood a man—at least, she assumed it was a man—clutching a huge teddy bear in one hand and a plastic orange tulip (which he appeared to be sniffing) in the other. On top of his pumpkin-shaped head was a hat-cum-umbrella. "I'm Mr. Maggs," he said softly, smiling a shark's teeth smile. "What brings you to my neck of the woods? This is private property. *Very* private property. You're trespassing on the Lyons family estate—well, *my* estate now, actually—little girl."

"I'm sorry, sir," said Le Fay ever so politely as her brain worked overtime to come up with an excuse for being in Fishbone Forest.

"Mr. Maggs."

"I beg your pardon?" asked Le Fay.

"Call me Mr. Maggs."

"I'm sorry, *Mr. Maggs*," said Le Fay. "My dog got off its leash and through a gap in your railings. He must be in here somewhere."

"And the other two?" said Mr. Maggs, bending down to Le Fay's height. She gave an involuntary shudder. There was something otherworldly and creepy about this newcomer.

"Oh, the twins, you mean?" said Le Fay, realizing that Mr. Maggs must have spotted them all at some stage and that a lie involving Albie, Josh, and Jackie—and so as near to the truth as possible—was one she was more likely to carry off without slipping up. "They're my brothers. They've gone off looking for Jackie."

"Jackie being your dog that got off its leash?" said Mr. Maggs.

"Exactly, Mr. Maggs," said Le Fay breezily, trying to act as if she had nothing to hide.

One of the things that was bothering her about Mr. Maggs, quite apart from his appearance and the teddy *and* the plastic flower, of course, was that he wasn't behaving like a grown-up. In this situation, a normal grown-up might have threatened her with telling her parents or the police, or demanded to know what she was up to, or might have asked her how she got muddy, or told her that she'd catch her death of cold in her soaking clothes.

"A strange doggie, that," said Mr. Maggs. "I caught a glimpse of it a moment ago when I came around the corner. It looked more like a jackal to me."

"It's an all-sorts dog," said Le Fay. "A mongrel. We got it from the Dillington Street Shelter." The rain was pouring into her face. Her hair was plastered flat against her head, making it look like it had been drawn on her skin with a thick black felt-tip pen.

Mr. Maggs ignored her lies, and she felt sure that he could tell they were just that. "Did you know that in folklore, all over the world, the jackal is associated with the Devil? It is thought of as an *evil* beast."

Le Fay most certainly did know. When you had a sister who turned into a jackal, you found out as much about jackals as you could. Jackals did seem to have a nasty reputation, but Jackie had assured her that it was all bunkum and that she never had evil thoughts, even when she was in her jackal form.

"I think that's a load of superstitious nonsense," said Le Fay. "Anyway, I don't believe in the Devil."

Mr. Maggs grinned at her, his face nicely dry under his umbrella hat. "But what if the Devil believes in you?" he asked.

Le Fay was flummoxed by that. "Are you going to throw me out or let me help my brothers look for my dog?" she said. "Either way, I need shelter from the rain."

"Which is why you're coming back to the house with me."

"The house?" asked Le Fay.

"There's a house here in the forest. It was built by the Lyons family. The Lyonses were also the ones who planted this forest."

"Oh . . . I didn't know that," said Le Fay.

"Well, that's where we're going," he said. "It'll take a while."

"I don't think so," said Le Fay. "My father said that I'm not to talk to strangers."

She felt Mr. Maggs grip her arm. "I'm not *asking* you," he said. There was an air of menace in his voice for the first time. "That's where we're going."

Despite all that wet everywhere, Le Fay's mouth went dry. "Okay," she said in a tiny voice.

When they finally reached and entered Fishbone Hall, after a soaking walk amongst the dreadful trees, Toby gave Le Fay an old blue terry-cloth robe to wear and a towel to dry her hair. Mr. Maggs had said something about having some business to attend to and then left the two of them alone.

"Thank you," said Le Fay, rubbing her hair with the towel. She stood by an old-fashioned wood-burning stove and looked around the room. A large hole in the ceiling gave her a glimpse into a bedroom above. A hole in the outer wall looked out onto the skeletal trees. "You live in this ruin?" she asked.

"Sure," said Toby. "My room's pretty dry in all weather."

"Is Mr. Maggs a relative or something?"

Toby laughed. "No way. He's the boss . . . or the *master*, as he likes to be called."

"That makes it sound like he owns you," said Le Fay. She hung the towel around her neck, like a boxer entering the ring, and held her hands in front of the stove. Her ribs still hurt when she moved.

"You should get out of those wet things," said Toby. "You're shivering."

"Well, would you mind leaving the room while I change?" asked Le Fay. "It's the polite thing to do."

Toby shook his head. "Sorry," he said. "No can do. I'm not allowed to leave you alone."

"I'm a prisoner?"

Toby avoided eye contact. He busied himself by picking up a CD from a small stack of them on a table (which had ivy growing up its legs) and slotting it into the

Discman clipped to his belt. "Mr. Maggs would say that you're a guest, but I suppose you are . . . a prisoner, I mean."

"Then turn around," said Le Fay.

Toby turned away from her and Le Fay stepped behind a freestanding bookcase for extra cover and slipped out of her wet clothes and into the blue terry-cloth robe. She also slipped a large glass paperweight into the robe pocket. Toby was bigger than she was, and Mr. Maggs was MUCH bigger than she was, and she'd never tried hitting anyone with anything, but she felt that tiny bit

safer having a weapon of sorts . . . should the time come when she needed one.

Le Fay hung her clothes on the back of a broken wooden chair, which she placed in front of the stove. "You'd better find a way to get me out of here or you're going to wind up in big trouble too," she said matter-of-factly.

"What do you mean?" asked Toby.

"I mean my dad's a war hero and his best friend is a detective called Charlie Tweedy, who is one of the most famous policemen in the country. . . ."

"So?" asked Toby, looking unimpressed.

"So when I don't show up at home later on, they're going to come looking for me in the forest, and when they find out you and Mr. Maggs have kidnapped me, you're going to be in big trouble."

"Somehow I don't think your father and his cop friend know that you're in Fishbone Forest," sneered Toby. Suddenly he looked a lot less friendly to Le Fay. "This is just the kind of place that policemen warn little kids away from."

That had, of course, been the main fault in Le Fay's lie. The fact that Le Fay's father had a wooden leg and that Charlie Tweedy had long since retired from the police force — sorry, *service* — had been easily glossed over. "Are you prepared to take that chance?" she challenged.

Toby walked right up to Le Fay, who was standing by an old oval table with a chipped milk jug on it being used as a vase. It was filled with a bunch of different-colored plastic tulips, like the one Mr. Maggs had been carrying outside. She pulled out a yellow flower and twirled the green plastic-coated wire stem between her fingers.

"However much of a fighting man your dad is, and however tough a cop Tweedy is, I'd rather take them on than Mr. Maggs any day," he said.

"Has he ever hurt you?" asked Le Fay.

"Me, hurt Toby?" said Mr. Maggs, who was suddenly standing at Le Fay's shoulder. Neither Toby nor Le Fay had seen or heard him enter the room. Le Fay jolted with surprise. "I'm a big pussycat." He pulled the plastic flower from Le Fay's grasp. "What do a madman, a poor man, and plastic tulips like these have in common?" he asked, that extraordinary grin of his spreading across his face.

"I—I—er—pardon?" said Le Fay.

"It's one of the master's riddles," Toby explained. "He likes a good riddle, now that things have turned out so well."

"I do indeed," said Mr. Maggs.

"All I want is to find Jackie and my brothers and get out of here," said Le Fay, digging her hands into the pockets of her borrowed robe and clutching the hidden glass paperweight for comfort.

"It's what *I* want that matters right now," said Mr. Maggs, tremblings of rage in his voice. "A madman, a poor man, and plastic tulips such as these . . . I'll give you a clue." He thrust the fake flower into Le Fay's face. "Sniff."

Le Fay was wise enough not to argue. She sniffed. "I can't smell anything," she said.

"Exactly." Mr. Maggs beamed.

"It's plastic. It has no scent."

"Exactly," Mr. Maggs repeated.

"I know! I know!" said Toby excitedly.

"Of course you know, you idiot. I've told you the answer before. But can this one work it out for herself, all on her own?"

"It's a pun!" said Le Fay, strangely pleased that she'd just guessed the answer despite the circumstances. "Plastic flowers like these have no scents . . . a poor man has no cents. . . ."

"And the MADMAN?"

"Has no *sense*."

"Splendid," said Mr. Maggs. Then he sighed. "What a pity you're the enemy!"

Le Fay looked into his eyes. He actually looked sad.

"I'm not your enemy," Le Fay insisted. "I'm a kid looking for a dog that got off its leash, that's all. . . ."

"If only that were true."

A moment later the door opened and in marched Albie, Josh, and Jackie (back in her human form), followed by Mulch. They dripped water onto the flagstone floor.

"Aaaaaaaaaah!" said Mr. Maggs, kissing his teddy on the nose. "The more the merrier!"

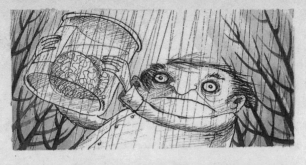

CHAPTER EIGHT

Mulch might not have been the brightest person in the world, let alone in Fishbone Forest that day, but as he ran through the mud and trees in the pouring rain, a thought occurred to him. The almost-identical twins, with their fierce-looking dog, seemed to care a great deal about the brain in the jar of pickling vinegar, so, rather than running, he would issue them an ultimatum. Which is why he finally stopped running.

Jackie the jackal bounded forward.

"Call the dog off or I smash the jar here and now!" Mulch commanded.

Albie looked at Josh. Josh looked at Albie. They knew that big sister Jackie would make that decision, but they couldn't tell the man that.

"Here—"

"—Jackie," they commanded, waiting to see how Jackie might respond.

She obviously took Mulch's threat seriously, because she trotted back to their side.

"Good!" said Mulch, trying to sound as tough as possible. "I want you out of here NOW, or I destroy this brain you seem so interested in."

"You can't do that," said Josh.

"Please," said Albie.

"You're weird, you know that? It ain't healthy, two young kids being interested in brains and the like. . . . You've put yourself in grave danger."

At the word *danger* Jackie dashed off into the trees, her tail held high.

"Jackie!" cried the twins as one. Surely she wasn't going to leave them alone with this strange man? Or had she suddenly gotten worried about them having left Le Fay on her own?

"I did warn you," said Mulch. "But now I'm going to have to let the master decide what we do with you."

"The master?" asked Albie.

"Is there a school around here or something?" asked Josh. Come to think of it, the man with the jar did remind him a little bit of the janitor at their school.

"Wait and see," said Mulch. "He might even let you keep the brain. . . . But remember, one false move from either of you and I flatten it like an overcooked cauliflower."

The boys reluctantly began to follow Mulch. After about ten minutes, Jackie stepped out in front of them, back in human form.

"Not another one of you!" groaned Mulch, for although

Jackie didn't have the same gappy teeth as Albie, Josh, and Le Fay, there was no mistaking that she was a relative: Her red hair and freckles instantly gave the game away. "This place is getting busier than Houser Point!" (Which would be like a Londoner saying "busier than Piccadilly Circus" or a New Yorker saying "busier than Grand Central Station.")

"What's going on?" asked Jackie, pretending, of course, that this was the first time she'd come face-to-face with Mulch rather than simply the first time she'd met him whilst she was in human form.

"You and the boys—" began Mulch.

"Joshua," said Albie.

"Albion," said Josh.

"All three of you are coming with me to the hall to meet the master, and he'll decide what we're going to do. If you try anything funny or that dog of yours comes within ten feet of me, I'm tipping this brain out of the jar."

"We don't want any trouble," said Jackie calmly. She'd gone back to the spot where they'd come through the railings, turned back into her original form, and changed into her clothes from the duffel bag. She'd also found that Le Fay was missing and that there was a faint scent of her and someone they hadn't run into yet. Someone who smelled very odd indeed. The big problem was the rain, though. It was washing away the scent trails, which meant that Jackie might get as lost as the rest of them . . . so she'd gone back to the twins.

And now all of them were in the relative dry of Fishbone Hall. And there was Le Fay, with the most extraordinary "man" Jackie'd ever seen and a goofy teenager in an XXL T-shirt that was much too big for him.

"Look what the Mulch dragged in." Toby grinned.

Le Fay wasn't nearly as frightened now that they were all together, especially when they had one really great trick up their sleeve — a great secret weapon, if you like — and she wasn't thinking of the paperweight in her robe pocket. What Mr. Maggs, Toby, and the funny little man they called Mulch didn't know was what Jackie could turn into. They not only outnumbered Mr. Maggs and the others four to three, but one of them could become a vicious dog in seconds! If it wasn't for the fact that the McNallys had to get back Fergal's brain, they could probably escape from Fishbone Hall there and then, though getting out of the forest might be harder. Mr. Maggs had the distinct advantage of knowing his territory.

Le Fay, Jackie, Albie, and Josh sat side by side, in that order, on a large old sofa with lumpy cushions and horse-hair stuffing sprouting through worn patches in the arms and back.

Mr. Maggs was pacing up and down in front of them, weaving between stone pillars, a roaring fire behind him. "What am I to do with you?" he mused.

"Simple," said Jackie. "Lend us an umbrella and show us a way out of the forest."

"What about your missing jackal? I beg your pardon . . . your missing *dog*?" asked Mr. Maggs.

"All the better if you help us find her," said Jackie, "but after the way you've been behaving, I assumed the sooner we were off your property the better."

Mr. Maggs stopped pacing and looked at her. His enormous teddy, tucked under his arm, seemed to look at her too. "My, you're good," he said. "Very clever. What's your name?"

"Sis," Le Fay blurted out. "She's called Sis!" She didn't want her sister calling herself Jackie when that was the name she'd told Mr. Maggs was the name of their missing dog.

"Hmmm," hmmmed Mr. Maggs.

"Nice place you've got here, Mr. M.," said Albie hurriedly.

"Could do with patching up here and there," said Josh.

"But with a bit of filler and a lick of paint it could be as right as—"

"—rain. Yours, is it?"

Mr. Maggs suddenly looked very pleased with himself. "Yes." He nodded. He'd obviously been irritated by the twins' chirpy interlude but was now satisfied that the question had given him a chance to show off. "Yes, it is mine. This forest, the house, and the huge fortune that goes with it have been in the Lyons family for years— *hundreds* of years—but Lionel Lyons was the last of the Lyons line and he died without issue."

"Without what?" asked Le Fay.

"Without tissues," said Joshua.

"No, not without tissues, without *issue*," Mr. Maggs corrected him. "What I mean is that he had no son and heir. He had no one to leave this place to . . . no one to leave the family fortune to. No relative, that is."

"He died without making a will," said Mulch, who had been listening at a respectful distance while tending to the fire.

"And left everything to me." Mr. Maggs beamed.

Mulch put another log on the fire with a large pair of brass tongs.

"That doesn't make sense," said Le Fay. "One minute Mulch says that Lionel Lyons died without a will and the next minute you say that he left you everything."

"Let's say that he put in a final appearance and made me his heir. It was an . . . an especially arranged appearance."

Of course, what the McNallys didn't know was that Mr. Maggs had deliberately befriended Lionel Lyons, that he had cultivated a friendship with the express purpose of convincing the tired and lonely eccentric old man, living in the middle of the forest, to leave the family fortune to him. And it had all been going so well until Lionel Lyons had simply died of old age when Mr. Maggs had been treating him to an ice cream one day.

What the McNallys didn't know was that Mr. Maggs had needed Lionel Lyons alive to make him his heir to the fortune in front of witnesses and, most importantly, go with him to the law firm of Garland & Fudge — always written with a squiggly & sign like that (which is called an ampersand, by the way, although it wasn't a Mr. Amper who invented it) rather than written out *a-n-d* — who had always dealt with Lyons family business.

What the McNallys didn't know was that Mr. Maggs had, therefore, stored the late Lionel Lyons on ice until — after some years of trial and error and much planning — he'd developed a way of apparently "bringing Lionel Lyons back to life" by placing a fresh brain in his lifeless body (well, *head*, actually) and that Mulch had stolen Fergal's brain for just that purpose, only to have it rejected by Mr. Maggs, who settled for the brain of a schoolteacher (who taught French) provided by his cousin Ralphie.

What the McNallys didn't know was that Mr. Maggs's harebrained scheme had worked. That after much confusion and some coaching in his new role, his patient had played his part perfectly. In the eyes of the (hoodwinked) law, Mr. Maggs was now the rightful owner of Fishbone Forest, Fishbone Hall, and, far more importantly to him, the Lyons millions.

"And after this special final appearance, you somehow ended up with the Lyons fortune?" asked Jackie from the middle of the sofa.

"I did."

"So, if now you're so rich, why are you still living in this dump—"

"—this place?" asked the twins.

Mr. Maggs perched himself on the arm of the sofa nearest to Josh and sat his teddy on his knee. "The money is not to be spent on trivial things such as a roof over my head or fancy meals!" he said. "I need the money for a far more important project. . . . It is for a far higher purpose."

"What—" said Albie.

"—purpose?" said Josh.

Le Fay thought of Fergal's brain in a jar and remembered the faint whiff of pickling vinegar. "Yes, Mr. Maggs," asked Le Fay. "What is it, exactly, that you want?"

CHAPTER NINE

"What is it, exactly, that I want?" roared Mr. Maggs, a terrible grin spreading across his almost human features. He gave his bald teddy a special hug. This was the question he had been waiting for. This was the question he'd been building up to for years of his extraordinary life. "What I want are *changes*," he declared. "Changes!"

As if to punctuate the point, he jumped up off the arm of the sofa and pushed against one of the huge ivy-clad pillars, which crumbled and fell onto the cold stone floor in an impressive pile of dust.

"And you shall have them, master," said Mulch and Toby in unison, like an official response in some bizarre religious ritual, only slightly spoiled by the odd cough and splutter caused by the clouds of pulverized masonry.

The pushing of the pillar had been an impressive feat, but this was an old house, much of it without so much as a roof and much of it crumbling stone. Le Fay reckoned that if *she'd* pushed that pillar hard enough, she too could have reduced it to rubble. "What kind of changes?" she demanded, fearing the worst. Le Fay wasn't familiar with the word *megalomaniac*, but if she had been, she'd have probably used it to describe this *being* standing before them now, half in shadow.

Mr. Maggs tucked his teddy under an arm and, with a clawlike hand, reached for a huge leather-bound book lying flat on a stone shelf. Pieces of paper of every conceivable shape and size were sticking out from between its pages, acting as markers: newspaper clippings, old bus tickets, folded paper bags, Post-it notes, torn strips of tissue paper, and even twisted foil once covering exciting chocolate mints. He opened the book just over halfway through, at a place marked by an old label soaked off a jar of marmalade.

"This is my *Manifesto of Change*," he declared. "These are my demands. . . . " The McNallys waited with fear in their hearts. What diabolical plan did he have for those around him . . . perhaps for humankind? "Change Number One," said Mr. Maggs. "The letter Q shall come later in the alphabet, to appear nearer X, Y, and Z."

There was a period of silence.

Jackie was stunned.

To be honest, she'd been expecting Mr. Maggs's demands to be for a limitless supply of slave labor or control over four continents. "Th-that sounds fair enough," she said at last.

"Two. A biopic of my life will be made, in which I shall be played by Cary Grant," said Mr. Maggs, turning his face into the light, as though showing his best side to some nonexistent camera.

"What's a biopic?" asked Joshua.

"Who's Cary Grant?" asked Albie.

"A biopic is a biographical picture," said Le Fay. "A movie about someone's life."

"And Cary Grant was a famous movie star," explained Jackie. "The only trouble is he died years ago, Mr. Maggs."

"Change Number Three," Mr. Maggs continued, ignoring them. "Cary Grant is no longer dead."

"Oh," said Jackie. "And Number Four?"

"That Christmas trees be drawn accurately on Christmas cards. They're nearly always drawn with the branches growing downward from the trunk when, in real life, they grow up."

"I'm not sure what you mean," confessed Jackie. Mr. Maggs turned around the book he was reading from so that she could take a look at an old Christmas card he'd stuck in it. The picture seemed to show a typical Christmas tree, in a snowy wood, its branches growing downward.

"Does that look right to you?" He glowered, his blackest of black pupils glinting like a bird's in the strange light.

"Y-Yes, I think so," said Jackie.

"Well, you thought wrong," said Mr. Maggs, and he flipped over the page to show a black-and-white photograph of a Christmas tree, torn from a newspaper and stuck into his book with old Band-Aids.

Jackie studied the photo. Mr. Maggs was right. Whereas the branches in the photo sprouted up like a **V**, the ones

in the drawing pointed down like a Λ (whatever that's called). "Wow!" she said, genuinely impressed. "I never noticed that before. I wonder why people so often draw them incorrectly?"

"They won't when the master's changes are implemented," said Mulch proudly.

Mr. Maggs turned back the book his way and turned the page again. "Change Number Five," he read. "Salt and pepper shall no longer be known by the collective term *cruet*."

"Cruet?" said Albie. "I've never heard it called that." They didn't have salt and pepper pots or shakers back home anyway.

"Me neither," said Josh.

Le Fay seemed miles away. She was still muttering something about "Change Number Three."

"You've never heard the term *cruet*?" asked Mr. Maggs.

They all—except Le Fay—shook their heads. "Oh lucky, lucky children!" he said, wiping a tear from his far-from-human eye with his teddy's paw. "When my changes have been made, we will live in a world where no one will have to hear salt and pepper referred to in that way again."

Albie leaned across to Jackie and whispered in her ear, "He's quite mad, you know, Jacks."

Joshua leaned across to his big sister and whispered, "He's nuttier than a bag of nuts with extra nuts in it, Jacks."

Worried that Mr. Maggs might overhear the twins' comments and become enraged and do something nasty, she loudly asked what Change Number Six would be.

"Ah," said Mr. Maggs with a contented smile. "Sums will be easier. All numbers will become even so that everything divides neatly into the other without complicated remainders and fractions and the like. Three will be an even number, so will seven, nine, eleven and so on. . . ."

"But that's ridiculous," said Le Fay, her mind back on the there and then (which was at the time, of course, the here and now). "Just because you say something *is*, doesn't make it so!" The minute she said it, she regretted it, but she couldn't take it back.

Mr. Maggs was trembling. He was most reminiscent of the early stages of an earthquake or of the initial rumblings of a volcano about to erupt, sending tremors across the flagstone floor of Fishbone Hall. His teddy bear's floppy limbs trembled under his arm. The book shook in his hands, one or two pieces of paper losing their place and fluttering to the floor. A snarl . . . a roar . . . something was beginning to form in his throat and his eyes somehow grew even wider and even darker.

The McNally children felt afraid, each and every one of them, even Jackie.

"I'm sure she meant no harm, master," said Mulch, hurrying to his side, actually stroking one of Mr. Maggs's arms in an effort to soothe him.

"N-n-no harm at all," Le Fay added hurriedly.

"Tell them about Change Number Seven, master," said Mulch. "They'll be interested in Number Seven."

Mr. Maggs shook Mulch free of his arm, an act that sent the little man flying across the room, where he crashed into the edge of a table with a terrible crunch and a groan. He gave off a little whimper and touched his head where he'd hit the floor. There was blood on his fingers. Toby giggled. Le Fay felt a pang of guilt. The nasty little man had only been trying to protect them from his master's wrath . . . a wrath caused by her contradicting him.

"Ah, yes, Change Number Seven," said Mr. Maggs, Mulch apparently as forgotten as a swatted fly and his near rage down to a simmer rather than actually boiling over. "Red wine will taste more like raspberry juice. At the moment it looks so nice, but doesn't taste nearly as good as the raspberry juice of my childhood, still warm from the sun."

"Splendid!" said Le Fay, rather overenthusiastically, trying to make up for past mistakes.

"Sounds good—"

"—to us," said Albie and Josh, respectively. Neither had ever drunk red wine *or* raspberry juice but imagined raspberry juice would be rather nice, so it didn't matter to them if red wine tasted that way.

"One of my personal favorites," said Mulch, getting to his feet, a neatly folded handkerchief pressed over the cut on his forehead.

"I'm rather fond of Number Eight," sneered Mr. Maggs, "but first let me see if you have been paying attention to the first seven. I'd hate to feel you were being disrespectful and not giving me your full attention. Line up!" He placed the book back on the shelf and hugged his teddy to his chest, the bear staring at the McNallys with his glass eyes.

Jackie, Le Fay, Albie, and Josh got to their feet and shuffled into line like a row of students before a teacher.

"Number One?" he demanded, pointing at Jackie.

"To make Q nearer the end of the alphabet, in amongst X, Y, and Z."

"Number Two?" Mr. Maggs pointed to the next in line.

"Cary Grant to play you in a movie about your life," said Le Fay.

"Good. Number Three?"

"Er, to bring Cary Grant back to life?" said Albie.

"Number Four?" demanded Mr. Maggs, looming over Josh.

"Er . . . er . . ." Joshua frantically tried to remember; then, thankfully, the answer popped into his head. "Trees!

Christmas trees must be drawn the right way, with branches pointing up, not down!"

"Five."

"Cruet!" Jackie blurted, having worked out she'd be asked this one and having the answer ready in the hope of pleasing the master . . . Mr. Maggs, that is. He was no master of the McNallys; not if Jackie had anything to do with it.

"Six?"

"No more fractions," began Albie.

"All numbers even," began Josh.

"SILENCE!" Mr. Maggs demanded. He spoke with such authority that no one dared speak.

"I was asking YOU," he said, prodding Le Fay with his teddy's paw, clutched in his long-nailed fingers that looked more like a cluster of gnarled twigs than a hand.

"Easier sums," she announced, keeping her cool in the way she had in the Tap 'n' Type competition at the hotel where Fergal had fallen from the window and died.

"Number Seven?"

"Red wine to taste more like raspberry juice!" said the McNallys as one.

Mr. Maggs positively beamed. His grin was as wide as a cartoon grin, much wider than any human being could achieve, showing off his extraordinarily pointed little teeth in all their glory. His head made Le Fay think of a pumpkin with shark's teeth, though not something she'd ever seen in real life.

"And so to Number Eight," said Mr. Maggs. "Ban beards without mustaches. All beards must be accompanied by a mustache at all times."

"Great idea," said Joshua.

"It's got my vote," said Albie. Neither of them knew what on Earth he was on about.

Mr. Maggs patted both the twins on the head at the same time, in the self-conscious way that no one who's used to children being around ever does. Suddenly he seemed to be behaving like a nice enough person, but the twins weren't fooled. This teddy-bear-clutching thing was no man, let alone a *nice* one. "Ahhhhh," he sighed.

"Mr. Maggs?" said Le Fay as cautiously and politely as possible.

"Yes, Le Fay, what is it?" Her name sounded exotic and different coming from his mouth.

"These changes . . . have you done anything to prepare for them . . . ?" She struggled for the right words. ". . . To make them happen when the time comes?"

"You mean, have I made preparations for implementing

them, such as printing alphabet books with the letters in their new order or—"

"Or looking for ways of bringing that movie star you were talking about—"

"Cary Grant," said Jackie helpfully.

"Of bringing Cary Grant back to life?" said Le Fay.

The strange and mighty Mr. Maggs crouched down and leaned forward so that his sweet breath blew into Le Fay's face as he spoke. "You are interested in reanimation?" he asked with obvious interest.

"Reanimation?" said Le Fay.

"Isn't that something to do with drawing?" asked Albie.

"Shhh!" said Jackie with a stern look.

"Reanimation is giving back life to something that has died," said Mulch from the shadowy corner of the room he was now occupying, at a safe distance from his master. "Animation is movement . . . is *life*."

Mr. Maggs ignored his minion. "When Cary Grant retired, a newspaper reporter was writing a story about him and wanted to check how old he was," he said. "So the reporter sent a telegram to Cary Grant's agent. Telegrams were typed messages and you paid by the word, so the message was short. It read: HOW OLD CARY GRANT? Cary Grant himself sent the reply. And do you know what he said? It read: OLD CARY GRANT FINE. HOW YOU?" Mr. Maggs threw back his head and laughed. "Old Cary Grant fine!"

Jackie laughed politely.

"Have you tried to reanimate him . . . to reanimate

anyone?" asked Le Fay, once the strange laughter had subsided.

Mr. Maggs's face became serious, deadly serious. "I might have, but that would be my business, wouldn't it? The kind of business where meddlers may find themselves in serious trouble if they tried to interf—"

Mr. Maggs was interrupted by a dog—a very friendly and bedraggled dog—which bounded in from the rain through one of the many gaping holes in the wall of Fishbone Hall.

On seeing the McNallys, he leapt up at Le Fay, causing her to wince with pain where she'd hurt her ribs, and covered her robe with muddy paw prints, his licky tongue giving her slobbery doggie kisses.

Before Mr. Maggs had a chance to speak, Mulch had dashed across the room, past the remains of the crumbled pillar, and grabbed the dog by his collar, pulling him off Le Fay.

The dog yelped and, turning his attention to the twins, wagged his tail furiously.

"I thought I told you that you could only keep the mutt if you kept it out of my sight!" said Mr. Maggs. "Get it out of here."

Mulch managed to drag the dog from the room, but it took two hands and a great deal of effort.

CHAPTER TEN

For reasons that will become apparent, I don't know what Mr. Maggs had in store for the McNallys. He hadn't asked them to come into Fishbone Forest. That had been their own doing. He hadn't lured them there or tricked them into coming. No one can accuse him of that. It was a twist of fate that had brought them together: He had needed a brain and Mulch had stolen Fergal's for that purpose. You can understand why Mr. Maggs didn't want people around when he was busy "reanimating" Lionel Lyons and tricking the lawyers into giving him the Lyons fortune, but all of this had been achieved before the McNallys arrived, and the evidence—well, *most* of it—was destroyed or long gone. So why didn't he simply have Toby or Mulch take Jackie, Le Fay, and the twins to one of the exits of Fishbone Forest and tell them never to come back?

Perhaps the answer lies in the way he hugged that teddy bear of his and enjoyed asking riddles. Perhaps what he really craved more than anything in his *Manifesto of Change* was *company*. Was the "Cousin Ralphie" who sent him the brain of the French teacher—who, incidentally, had died in a boating accident—really his cousin? Did this extraordinary being really have a family? He certainly didn't seem to have any friends. Mulch and Toby were there because they worked for him, and he was a strict master.

And why share his manifesto with complete strangers? After all, he didn't have any idea that it was their dead brother's brain that had led their paths to cross.

Perhaps it wasn't company for company's sake that he craved. Perhaps he needed an audience, an audience to show off to? Because he didn't have family or friends around him, he didn't really have a chance to polish up his social skills. To put it another way: He wasn't very good with people. Not being a person himself no doubt made it all the harder.

If Mr. Maggs kept the McNallys in Fishbone Hall at the heart of Fishbone Forest, they could be his captive audience. He could impress them with his manifesto and his riddles as much as he liked. Maybe that was what he intended. As I've said before, we'll never know for sure. Why? Because the holes were active again.

In the USA, running all the way from San Francisco to the hills behind Los Angeles, is a geological feature called the San Andreas Fault. It's what geologists call a "strike-slip fault," which means that a fracture in the earth's crust— way, *way* down there—causes horizontal movement in the ground near the surface. The San Andreas Fault is nearly always tremoring and twitching (like a dog's legs when it's dreaming about chasing cars or rabbits), but sometimes it causes big, big earthquakes. One of these quakes was so big that it destroyed much of the city of San Francisco in 1906.

Now, the question you might be asking yourself is this: If people know that the fault's there and the damage it can cause to property and lives, why does anyone in their right mind live there? And the answer lies in the fact that we all take chances. Look at it this way: You're more likely to fall out of an airplane if you're in an airplane in the first place. You're more likely to be killed crossing the road if you cross roads, but these are chances we're willing to take. To most people, the advantages of flying in aircraft outweigh the disadvantages. If you never crossed roads, your movements would be severely restricted. People live and work on the San Andreas Fault for a whole variety of reasons, and though they think about the possibility of earthquakes, they don't think about them all the time; they don't let the earthquakes rule their lives.

It was rather like that in the country where the McNallys lived (and as I made very clear in the previous exploit, wherever you think that country is, you're wrong). The recent outbreak of holes had started out as big news but very quickly became just another of "those things," to be lived with until it touched your particular life.

Fergal, Jackie, and the twins had encountered a fresh hole when they'd been on their way to The Dell (the hotel from which Fergal eventually fell). If the bus they'd been in had arrived at that spot a few minutes earlier, they'd probably all have ended up in it as it opened up beneath them.

They'd all seen the hole in Garland Park, and that was a really big one, but it had been there a few days before the McNallys had come across it, and the authorities had already cordoned it off. Holes touched the edges of their lives but were never center stage. Until now.

Mulch dragged the dog back out into the rain, around the side of the Hall, and into one of the outbuildings. This small building had been as ruinous as the main house in places, but Mulch had bricked up the holes in the walls as best he could and patched the roof with carpet swatches. The truth be told, it was now warmer and drier than his own room. This was where he kept the dog.

Mulch had grown very fond of the mongrel since he'd knocked the poor creature down with his English-mustard-colored van and then nursed him back to life. He had no way of knowing that he had belonged to Wanda de Vere and was called Bumbo because there'd been no tag on his collar.

He and the animal got on very well after Mulch had done everything possible to put things right and make him well again. He'd even performed surgery. Part of him wanted to tell Mr. Maggs, to show off his handiwork and to say "Why can't I be the one to help you perform any operations in the future and not Toby?" But part of him knew that Mr. Maggs would be angry if he knew what he'd done. So he kept quiet about the accident, and only when the dog was well again did he tell his master that he'd found him loose in the forest and ask to keep him. Mr. Maggs had agreed, so long as it never came into the house.

The dog was behaving very oddly. Normally he was simply pleased to see Mulch and jumped up at him and stared deep into his eyes (though he had never licked him in the way he had licked Le Fay), but now he was struggling to get away from Mulch again.

"Please behave, boy," said Mulch, "or you'll get us both into trouble. It's nice and cozy in here and you mustn't upset Mr. Maggs."

It's true. The outbuilding was cozy. Mulch had put plenty of dry straw on the floor, and there were two big bowls under the window, one filled with water and the other with dried dog food. The only other object in the room was a large jar in the corner. You know the one. It had a brain in it, in pickling vinegar.

The dog still struggled. "Please don't make me tie you up," said Mulch. As if he understood, the dog stopped struggling and looked up at Mulch. Mulch rubbed his head between the ears. "I'll be back later," he said.

Back in the rain, Mulch pulled the door shut behind him and made sure that the latch was down properly this time so that the dog couldn't get out again. Then he hurried back into the Hall.

He found Mr. Maggs trying to strike a bargain with the McNallys.

"It'll be completely dark soon," he was saying, "and you'll never find your way out of Fishbone Forest without my guidance, so I'd like you all to stay the night . . . as my guests."

The darkness would be no hindrance to Jackie in her jackal form. She could sniff her way out of there. If it wasn't for the rain. The rain changed everything.

"Guests?" said Albie.

"Prisoners, more like," said Josh.

"Our father and Detective Tweedy will already be wondering where we are," added Le Fay.

"Don't you understand?" said Mr. Maggs. "No one comes into the forest. No one. Missing animals. Missing people. It makes no difference. No one ventures here."

"We did," Jackie reminded him.

Mr. Maggs paused before answering, idly stroking the back of his teddy bear's head. "Yes, you four are different, there's no denying that . . . perhaps such different children do have a father different enough to come searching. I think I'll have to—"

And then it happened. We'll never know what Mr. Maggs had planned because the whole room started to shake so violently that a number of burning logs rolled out of the fire. Mulch grabbed a pillar, but it fell to the floor in great stone chunks.

Jackie instinctively put her arms around Albie and Josh to protect them, whilst Toby ran out of the building into the dark forest and the pouring rain. Le Fay lost her footing and ended up sprawled on the cold flagstones, winded once again and her ribs more painful still.

She watched in horror as the floor directly in front of her began to give way.

CHAPTER ELEVEN

As Mr. Maggs fell into the gaping void that was the hole that had opened up beneath him, he didn't let out a cry, but—unlike poor Fergal McNally, who'd made no sound—he began to sing.

Leaning over the edge, with arms outstretched in a futile bid to try to catch him—a reflex action to try to save a fellow living being—Le Fay could hear the words clearly. The others dashed forward. They heard something too. Was it possible? Were they imagining things? No, it really was Mr. Maggs's voice they heard as, clutching his beloved teddy to him, he fell to his inevitable death.

His voice was thin and reedy and the words to the old song strangely moving:

"Me and my teddy bear
Have no worries
Have no cares.
Me and my teddy bear
Just play and play
All daaaaaaaaaaaaaaaaaaaay!"

Then silence, the terrible silence that follows death. No rumbling. No singing. All was silent and still at the heart of the forest.

"Is everyone okay?" asked Jackie, after what seemed like an eternity. She got to her feet and brushed the dust and grime from her clothes.

Mulch was leaning over the hole, sobbing. "Poor master . . . poor, poor master."

"There's no way he survived that," said Jackie, no doubt thinking of Fergal's fall, just as the others must have been.

Albie and Josh put an arm around each of Mulch's shoulders and tried to comfort him.

"It sounds to me like he died happy," said Albie.

"And with his teddy," said Josh. "I reckon he'd . . . he'd have wanted that."

"He wasn't a bad man," sobbed Mulch, standing up slowly with his head bowed.

"He wasn't a man," Jackie reminded him, picking up Mr. Maggs's leather-bound book from the floor, it having narrowly missed the hole by a matter of millimeters. She threw the *Manifesto of Change* into the void after its author. Mulch made no effort to stop her. "Now he'll never be able to implement his changes."

"I don't think he would ever have been able to anyway," said Le Fay. "Not if he'd lived another hundred years. They'd have been kind of difficult to do."

"If anyone could, *he* could have," sobbed Mulch.

Jackie just wanted to get the others home. This was

the second death they'd witnessed. There was too much sadness in their short lives.

At that moment there was a barking noise, and for the second time that evening, the dog that had befriended Le Fay bounded through a hole in the wall and into the room. The tremors caused by the hole had not only lifted the door on the outbuilding off its latch but also off its hinges.

On seeing Jackie, Le Fay, and the twins, he yelped with utter delight and wagged his tail like a clockwork toy, leaping up at each of them in turn, licking their faces and pawing at them.

"He's not much of a guard dog, is he?" said Le Fay, scratching him between the ears. "I imagined Mr. Maggs would have a pit bull or a German shepherd."

"He wasn't a guard dog," said Mulch. "I don't know where he came from. . . . He was loose in the forest and ran straight in front of my van."

"You knocked him down?" asked Le Fay, looking at the neatly stitched wound on the dog's head as he licked her fingers with his big pink tongue, staring up at her with his big, goo-goo brown eyes.

Mulch nodded.

"Well, the vet's done a good job fixing him up," said Josh, trying not to think of Mr. Maggs lying at the bottom of that hole.

"He seems pretty happy," agreed Albie.

A look of pride appeared on Mulch's sad face. "I didn't take him to any vet," he explained. "I made him well again."

"Does he have a name?" asked Le Fay, whose knees were now getting a good clean from the licky dog's licky tongue.

"Fergus," said Mulch. "No, that's not right. Fergal. That's it. Fergal."

Silence.

Have you ever heard the saying that "the blood froze in someone's veins"? Of course, that's not literally what happens—well, certainly not to Jackie, Le Fay, Albie, and Josh—but that's what it felt like. They froze to the spot with a hot and cold tingling sensation all over.

They couldn't have been more stunned if someone had stabbed them with an icicle.

Mulch was surprised by the effect that he'd had on them. "What's wrong?" he demanded.

"Why . . . why did you call him Fergal?" asked Le Fay, her mouth completely dry. She could hear her own heart thumping in her chest. She watched the dog sit up on his hind legs, thumping his tail with glee at the mention of his name.

"It was the name of the person whose brain I put inside him," said Mulch at last. "Fergal McNally, Juvenile," he explained, remembering the exact wording on the pickling jar.

A moment later, the four McNallys threw themselves

at the dog, showering him with hugs and kisses, and he in turn licked off the tears of joy that were pouring down their faces.

Only Jackie was able to find the words: "You're coming with us, Fergal," she said. "We're taking you home."

It's ironic that the McNally family had so much to thank Stefan Multachan, the masked burglar, for. If he hadn't stolen Fergal's brain in the first place, Fergal—in any way, shape, or form—would have remained dead after his fall from The Dell's window. If later on, though, Mulch had done as Mr. Maggs had ordered, they would never have gotten Fergal back, and let me tell you, a four-legged little brother is better than none at all.

As you'll no doubt recall (if you didn't skip those pages), when Mr. Maggs's Cousin Ralphie supplied the French teacher's brain to "reanimate" Lionel Lyons's body, Mulch was told to "dispose" of Fergal's unwanted one. It had become redundant. Instead, he'd kept it in the jar, guilty at the thought of throwing away something once so precious.

When, after days in which the poor injured dog had gotten worse and worse and finally died—that's the last death I'll be mentioning in this exploit, though, of course, Mr. Maggs died after him, chronologically speaking—Mulch'd had the brain wave (no pun intended) of putting the brain from the jar inside the dog and the dog's old brain in the jar! It had, of course, been Bumbo's old brain he'd been carrying when he'd run into the McNallys in the forest.

Okay, so carrying out the operation had been more to do with wanting the dog back than wanting to preserve the memories of the juvenile human brain with the slight whiff of pickling vinegar, but using his master's techniques, he had, in fact, succeeded in bringing Fergal's mind back to life—full of all its love and feelings and memories right up until he'd hit the ground. *And* Mulch had the decency to name the mutt after him!

It had been a real puzzle for Fergal, of course, because he had no memories of being in a jar. To him, no time had passed since he'd hit the pavement and opened his eyes to find that he was a dog. After he realized that he really had turned into a dog (he didn't know anything about brain implants and reanimation at this stage, of course, though his family later explained everything), he assumed that it must either be his particular special power (turning into a dog when falling out of windows) or to do with reincarnation.

Fergal had read about it once: the belief that when you die, you come back as another animal. The better you were in your previous life, the "better" the animal you came back as. If you'd led your life like a skunk, you might come back as a skunk was how Fergal had reckoned it worked. Coming back as a dog didn't seem that bad. After all, he could have ended up a dung beetle or something!

The real frustration had been seeing Jackie, Le Fay, Albie, and Josh in Fishbone Hall and trying to tell them that he was Fergal and still alive, just in a new body! If only he could have made them understand. He couldn't speak. Sure, he could bark and whimper, but a dog's mouth isn't designed for human speech. It wasn't just that a dog's mouth doesn't have the lips to form the words; no matter how hard Fergal tried, he couldn't form any words in his throat either.

Now that the truth was out and he had his brothers and sisters around him, Fergal found himself doing a very doggy thing. He widdled/peed/weed with excitement. This was something Fergal never would have done and made him realize later, when he had a chance to think about it, that although it was his brain and his memories, it was Bumbo's blood flowing through his veins and

Bumbo's heart that was pumping it, so there would always be a little Bumbo in his behavior.

When Fergal was back home with his family, his father, Captain Rufus, didn't need much to convince him that this lovable mutt was his youngest boy.

He looked into the dog's eyes and said, "Welcome home, Fergal," and then gave him a big bowl of water to drink.

Then came the great discovery.

The only member of the McNally family not pleased to see the return of Fergal or, to be more technically accurate, to see the return of Fergal's brain, with all its memories, inside the body of what had been Bumbo, was Smoky the cat. She took one look at this dog that everyone was so delighted to see and her furry purry body turned to smoke, which drifted away, leaving nothing behind.

"So that's why Mum named her Smoky!" said Jackie. "Even our cat has hidden powers."

Of course, Smoky hadn't left. The smoke had re-formed into the big solid cat that she was in the other room, away from the smelly dog. It became Smoky's "party piece." Whenever Fergal came into the same room as her, she'd turn into smoke particles and drift off, ready to re-form. Her favorite destination was the top of a big old wardrobe in the bedroom. It was soon thick with cat hairs, like a strange nest!

That was a discovery, all right, but it wasn't *the* great discovery. The great discovery was that whenever Jackie turned into a jackal (which, as has been pointed out on more than one occasion, is little more than a kind of wild dog), she and Fergal found that they could communicate without speech. In that state, she could understand his doggie thoughts and later share them with the others.

This made Fergal's happiest times when he and his big sister could run wild on all fours, chasing each other in the moonlight, nipping at each other's furry tails and howling at the moon. Fergal—the *new* Fergal—was alive again, with all the adventures that life had to offer ahead of him. Which, as I've said on another occasion, about another matter, is all rather unlikely, isn't it?

In the middle of deep, dark Fishbone Forest, in the remains of Fishbone Hall, there was a deep, dark hole and at the bottom of that hole something stirred. It wasn't Mr. Maggs. It was a teddy bear, and it began its long crawl upward toward the light.

THE END

of the Second Exploit